YELLOW

W . W . NORTON & COMPANY

NEW YORK / LONDON

YELLOW

STORIES

DON LEE

For information about permission to reproduce selections from this book,
write to Permissions, W. W. Norton & Company, Inc.,
500 Fifth Avenue, New York, NY 10110.

The text of this book is composed in Sabon
with the display set in Regulator
Desktop composition by Molly Heron
Manufacturing by The Maple-Vail Book Manufacturing Group
Book design by JAM Design
Production manager: Andrew Marasia
Manuscript editor: David Cole

Library of Congress Cataloging-in-Publication Data

Lee, Don, 1959–
Yellow: stories / by Don Lee
p. cm.
Contents: the price of eggs in China—Voir dire—Widowers—
The lone night cantina—Casual water—The possible husband—
Domo arigato—Yellow.
ISBN 0-393-02562-4
1. California—Social life and customs—Fiction.
2. Asian Americans—Fiction. I. Title.

PS3562.E339 Y45 2001
813'.6—dc21

00-050047

W. W. Norton & Company, Inc.
500 Fifth Avenue, New York, N.Y. 10110

W. W. Norton & Company Ltd.
10 Coptic Street, London WCIA 1PU

2 3 4 5 6 7 8 9 0

For my father, Victor,
my sister, Teresa,
and in memory of
my mother, Jean

Thanks to my editor, Alane Salierno Mason, and my agent, Maria Massie; my friends who read the work over the years: David and Bethany Daniel, Heidi Pitlor, Fred Leebron, Kathryn Herold, Richard Haesler, Jennifer Egan, Debra Spark, Susan Conley, Melanie Rae Thon, Scott Buck, Mary Behrens, James Carroll, John Skoyles, and DeWitt Henry; the Massachusetts Cultural Council and the St. Botolph Club Foundation for fellowships; and the editors of the magazines in which these stories, in different form, first appeared: *The Gettysburg Review* ("The Price of Eggs in China"), *Glimmer Train* ("Voir Dire"), *GQ* ("Widowers," as "El Niño"), *Ploughshares* ("The Lone Night Cantina"), *New England Review* ("Casual Water" and "Domo Arigato"), and *American Short Fiction* ("Yellow").

CONTENTS

YELLOW

THE PRICE OF EGGS IN CHINA

I T WAS noon when Dean Kaneshiro arrived at Oriental Hair Poet No. 2's house, and as she opened the door, she said, blinking, "Hello. Come in. I'm sorry. I'm not quite awake."

He carried his measuring rig through the living room, noting the red birch floor, the authentic Stickley, the Nakashima table, the Maloof credenza—good craftsmanship, carefully selected, this poet, Marcella Ahn, was a woman who knew wood.

"When you called," she said in her study, "I'd almost forgotten. It's been over two years! I hope I wasn't too difficult to track down."

Immediately Dean was annoyed. When she had ordered the chair, he had been clear about his backlog, and today was the exact date he'd given her for the fitting. And she *had* been

1 3

difficult to track down, despite his request, two years ago, that she notify him of any changes of address. Her telephone number in San Francisco had been disconnected, and he had had to find her book in the library, then call her publisher in New York, then her agent, only to learn that Marcella Ahn had moved an hour south of San Francisco to the very town, Rosarita Bay, where he himself lived. Never mind that he should have figured this out, having overheard rumors of yet another Asian poet in town with spectacular long hair, rumors which had prompted the references to her and Caroline Yip, his girlfriend of eight months, as the Oriental Hair Poets.

He adjusted his rig. Marcella Ahn was thin and tall, but most of her height was in her torso, not her legs—typical of Koreans. She wore tight midnight-blue velvet pants, lace-up black boots, and a flouncy white Victorian blouse, her tiny waist cinched by a thick leather belt.

"Sit, please," he said. She settled into the measuring rig. He walked around her twice, then said, "Stand up, please." After she got up, he fine-tuned the back supports and armrests and shortened the legs. "Again, please."

She sat down. "Oh, that's much better, infinitely better," she said. "You can do that just by looking?"

Now came the part that Dean always hated. He could use the rig to custom-fit his chairs for every part of the body except for one. "Could you turn around, please?"

"Sorry?"

"Could you turn around? For the saddling of the seat?"

Marcella Ahn's eyes lighted, and the whitewash of her foundation and powder was suddenly broken by the mischievous curl of her lips, which were painted a deep claret. "You mean you want to examine . . . my *buttocks*?"

He could feel sweat popping on his forehead. "Please."

Still smirking, she raised her arms, the ruffled cuffs of her blouse dropping away, followed by the jangling release of two dozen silver bracelets on each wrist. There were silver rings on nearly every digit, too, and with her exquisitely lacquered fingers, she slowly gathered her hair—straight and lambent and hanging to midthigh—and raked it over one shoulder so it lay over her breast. Then she pivoted on her toe, turned around, and daintily lifted the tail of her blouse to expose her butt.

He squatted behind her and stared at it for a full ten seconds. It was a good butt, a firm, StairMastered butt, a shapely, surprisingly protuberant butt.

She peeked over her shoulder. "Need me to bend over a little?" she asked.

He bounced up and moved across the room and pretended to jot down some notes, then looked around. More classic modern furniture, very expensive. And the place was neat, obsessive-compulsive neat. He pointed to her desk. "You'll be using the chair here?"

"Yes."

"To do your writing?"

"Uh-huh."

"I'll watch you, then. For twenty minutes, please."

"What? Right now?"

"It'll help me to see you work, how you sit, maybe slouch."

"It's not that simple," she said.

"No?"

"Of course not. Poets can't write on demand. You know nothing about poetry, do you?"

"No, I don't," Dean said. All he ever read, in fact, were mystery novels. He went through three or four of them a week—anything with a crime, an investigation. He was now so familiar with forensic techniques, he could predict almost any plot twist, but his head still swam in delight at the first hint of a frame-up or double-cross.

He glanced out the window. Marcella Ahn lived off Skyview Ridge Road, which crested the rolling foothills, and she had one of the few panoramic views of Rosarita Bay—the harbor to the north, the marsh to the south, the town in the middle, and, everywhere beyond, the vast Pacific.

Marcella Ahn had her hands on her hips. "And I don't slouch," she said.

Eventually he did convince her to sit in her present desk chair, an ugly vinyl contraption with pneumatic levers and bulky ergonomic pads. She opened a bound notebook and uncapped a fountain pen, and hovered over the blank page for what seemed like a long time. Then she abruptly set everything aside and booted up her laptop computer. "What do you do with clients who aren't within driving distance?"

"I ask for a videotape, and I talk to their tailor. Try to work, please. Then I'll be out of your way."

"I feel so silly."

"Just pretend I'm not here," he said.

Marcella Ahn continued to stare at the computer screen. She shifted, crossed her legs, and tucked them underneath her. Finally, she set her fingers on the keys and tapped out three words—all she could manage, apparently. She exhaled heavily. "When will the chair be ready?"

"I'll start on it next month, on April twentieth, then three weeks, so May eleventh," he told her, though he required only half that time. He liked to plan for contingencies, and he knew his customers wanted to believe—especially with the prices they were paying—that it took him longer to make the chairs.

"Can I visit your studio?" she asked.

"No, you cannot."

"Ah, you see, you can dish it—"

"It would be very inconvenient."

"For twenty minutes."

"Please don't," he said.

"Seriously. I can't swing by for a couple of minutes?"

"No."

Marcella Ahn let out a dismissive puff. "Artists," she said.

⸱ ⸱ ⸱

ORIENTAL Hair Poet No. 1 was a slob. Caroline Yip lived in an apartment above the R. B. Feed & Hardware store, one small room with a Pullman kitchen, a cramped bathroom, and no closets. Her only furnishings were a futon, a boom box, and a coffee table, and the floor was littered with clothes, CDs, shoes, books, newspapers, bills, and magazines. There was a thick layer of grease on the stovetop, dust and hair and curdled food on every other surface, and the bathroom was clogged with sixty-two bottles of shampoo and conditioner, some half-filled, most of them empty.

Dean had stayed in the apartment only once—the first time

they had slept together. He had lain naked on her futon, and
Caroline had inspected his erection, baldly surveying it from
different angles. "Your penis looks like a fire hydrant," she
had said. "Everything about you is short, squat, and thick."
It was true. Dean was an avid weightlifter, not an ounce of fat
on him, but his musculature was broad and tumescent,
absent of definition. His forearms were pickle jars, almost as
big as his thighs, and his crewcutted head sat on his shoulders
without the relief of a neck. "What am I doing with you?"
Caroline said. "This is what it's come down to, this is how
far I've sunk. I'm about to fuck a Nipponese fire hydrant
with the verbal capacity of tap water."

There were other peculiarities. She didn't sleep well,
although she had done almost everything possible short of
psychotherapy—which she didn't believe in—to alleviate her
insomnia and insistent stress: acupuncture, herbs, yoga,
homeopathy, tai chi. She ran five miles a day, and she medi-
tated for twenty minutes each morning and evening, beginning her sessions by trying to relax her face, stretching and
contorting it, mouth yowling open, eyes bulging—it was a
horrific sight.

Even when she did sleep, it was fitful. Because she ground
her teeth, she wore a plastic mouthpiece to bed, and she bit
down so hard on it during the night, she left black spots
where her fillings were positioned. She had nightmares, a
recurring nightmare, of headless baby chickens chasing after
her, hundreds of decapitated little chicks tittering in rabid
pursuit.

The nightmares, however, didn't stop her from eating
chicken, or anything else, for that matter. She was a waif,

five-two, barely a hundred pounds. Her hair—luxuriant, butt-length, and naturally kinky, a rarity among Asians—seemed to weigh more than she did. Yet she had a ravenous appetite. She was constantly asking for seconds, picking off Dean's plate. "Where does it all go?" he asked over dinner one night, a month into their courtship.

"What?"

"The food."

"I have a very fast metabolism. You're not going to finish that?"

He scraped the rest of his portion into her bowl, and he watched her eat. He had surprised himself by how fond he'd become of her. He was a disciplined man, one with solitary and fastidious habits, yet Caroline's idiosyncrasies were endearing to him. Maybe this was the true measure of love, he thought—when you willingly tolerate behavior that, in anyone else, would be annoying, even abhorrent to you. Without thinking, he blurted out, "I love you."

"Yikes," Caroline said. She put her chopsticks down and wiped her mouth. "You are the sweetest man I know, Dean. But I worry about you. You're so innocent. Didn't anyone let you out of the house when you were young? Don't you know you're not supposed to say things like that so soon?"

"Do you love me?"

She sighed. "I don't right now," she said. Then she laid her hands on top of his head and shook it. "But I think I will. Okay, you big boob?"

It took her two more months to say that she might, maybe, be a little bit in love with him, too. "Despite everything, I guess I'm still a romantic," she said. "I will never learn."

They were both reclusive by nature, and most of the time were content to sequester themselves in Dean's house, which was tucked in a canyon in the coastal mountains. They watched videos, read, cooked Japanese dishes: *tonkatsu, oyako donburi, tempura, unagi.* It was a quiet life, free of catastrophe, and it had lulled Dean into thinking that there would be no harm in telling her about his encounter with Oriental Hair Poet No. 2.

"That cunt!" Caroline said. "That conniving Korean cunt! She's moved here on purpose!"

It was all she could talk about for three days. Caroline Yip and Marcella Ahn, it turned out, had a history. They had both lived in Cambridge, Massachusetts, in their twenties, and for several years they had been the best of friends—inseparable, really. But then their first books came out at the same time, Marcella's from a major New York publisher, Caroline's from a small, albeit respected press. Both had very similar jacket photos, the two women looking solemn and precious, hair flowing in full regalia. An unfortunate coincidence. Critics couldn't resist reviewing them together, mocking the pair, even then, as "The Oriental Hair Poets," "The Braids of the East," and "The New Asian Poe-tresses."

But Marcella came away from these barbs relatively unscathed. Her book, *Speak to Desire,* was taken seriously, compared to Marianne Moore and Emily Dickinson. Her poetry was highly erudite, usually beginning with mundane observations about birds or plant life, then slipping into long, abstract meditations on entropy and inertia, the Bible, evolution, and death, punctuated by the briefest mention of personal deprivations—anorexia, depression, abandonment. Or so the critics said. Dean still had the book from the library, but he couldn't make heads or tails of it.

In contrast, Caroline's book, *Chicks of Chinese Descent,* had been skewered. She wrote in a slangy, contemporary voice, full of topical, pop culture allusions. She wrote about masturbation and Marilyn Monroe, about tampons and *moo goo gai pan,* about alien babies and chickens possessed by the devil. She was roundly dispatched as a mediocre talent.

Worse, Caroline said, was what happened afterward. Marcella began to thwart her at every turn. Teaching jobs, coveted magazine publications, awards, residencies, fellowships—everything Caroline applied for, Marcella got. It didn't hurt that Marcella was a shameless schmoozer, flirting and networking with anyone who might be of use. Yet, the fact was, Marcella was rich. Her father was a shipping tycoon, and she had a trust fund in the millions. She didn't need any of these pitifully small sinecures which would have meant a livelihood to Caroline, and it became obvious that the only reason Marcella was pursuing them at all was to taunt her.

"She's a vulture, a vampire," Caroline told Dean. "You know she won't go out in the light of day? She stays up until four, five in the morning and doesn't wake up until past noon."

And then there was the matter of Evan Paviromo, the English-Italian editor of a literary journal whom Caroline had dated for seven years, waiting patiently for them to get married and have children. He broke it off one day without explanation. She dogged him. Why? Why was he ending it? She refused to let him go without some sort of answer. Finally he complied. "It's something Marcella said," he admitted.

At first Caroline feared they were having an affair, but the truth was more vicious. "Marcella told me she admired me," Evan said, "that I was far more generous than she could ever be. She said she just wouldn't be able to stay with someone whose work she didn't really respect. I thought about that, and I decided I'm not that generous. It's something that would eat away at me, that's bothered me all along. It's something I can't abide."

Caroline fled to California, eventually landing in Rosarita Bay. She completely disengaged herself from the poetry world. She was still writing every day, excruciating as it was for her, but she had not attempted to publish anything in six years. She was thirty-seven now, and a waitress—the breakfast shift at a diner, the dinner shift at a barbecue joint. Her feet had grown a full size from standing so much, and she was broke. But she had started to feel like her old self again, healthier, more relaxed, sleeping better. Dean had a lot to do with it, she said. She was happy—or as happy as it was possible for a poet to be. Until now. Until Marcella Ahn suddenly arrived.

"She's come to torment me," Caroline said. "Why else would she move to Rosarita Bay?"

"It's not such a bad place to live."

"Oh, please."

Dean supposed she was right. On the surface, Rosarita Bay looked like a nice seaside town, a rural sanctuary between San Francisco and Santa Cruz. It billed itself as the pumpkin capital of the world, and it had a Main Street lined with gas street lamps and old-time, clapboarded, saltbox shops and restaurants. Secluded and quiet, it felt like genuine small-town America, and most of the eight thousand residents preferred it that way, voting down every development plan that came down the pike.

Yet the things that gave Rosarita Bay its charm were also killing it. There were only two roads into town, Highway 1 on the coast and Highway 71 through the San Vicente Mountains, both of them just two lanes and prone to landslides. The fishing and farming industries were drying up, there were no new jobs, and, for those who worked in San Francisco or "over the hill" in San Vicente, it was a murderous, traffic-choked commute. The weather was also terrible, rain-soaked and wave-battered in the winter, wind-beaten in the spring, and fog-shrouded all summer long, leaving basically two good months—September and October.

In theory quaint and pretty, Rosarita Bay was actually a no-man's-land, a sleepy, slightly seedy backwater with the gray air of anonymity. People stuck to themselves, as if shied by failure and missed opportunities. You could get lost here, forgotten. It was, when all was said and done, a place of exile. It was not a place for a wealthy, jet-setting artiste and bon vivant like Marcella Ahn. But to come here because of Caroline? No. Dean could not believe it.

"How could she have even known you were here?" he asked Caroline. "You said you're not in touch with any of those people anymore."

"She probably hired a detective."

"Come on."

"You don't understand. I suppose you think if anyone's looking for revenge, it'd be me, that I can't be a threat to her because I'm such a loser."

"I wish you'd stop putting yourself down all the time. You're not a loser."

"Yes, I am. You're just too polite to say so. You're so fucking Japanese."

Early on, she had given him her book to read, and he had told her he liked it. But when pressed, he'd had to admit that he didn't really understand the poems. He was not an educated man, he had said.

"You pass yourself off as this simple chairmaker," Caroline said. "You were practically monosyllabic when we began seeing each other. But I know you're not the gallunk you make yourself out to be."

"I think you're talented. I think you're very talented." How could he explain it to her? Something had happened as he'd read her book. The poems, confusing as they were, had made his skin prickle, his throat thicken, random images and words—*kiwi, quiver, belly, maw*—wiggling into his head and taking residence.

"Are you attracted to her?" Caroline asked.

"What?"

"You're not going to make the chair for her, are you?"

"I have to."

"You don't have a contract."

"No, but—"

"You still think it's all a coincidence."

"She ordered the chair *sixteen months* before I met you."

"You see how devious she is?"

Dean couldn't help himself. He laughed.

"She has some sick bond to me," Caroline said. "In all this

time, she hasn't published another book, either. She *needs* me. She *needs* my misery. You think I'm being hysterical, but you wait."

I T began with candy and flowers, left anonymously behind the hardware store, on the stairs that led up to Caroline's apartment. Dean had not sent them.

"It's her," Caroline said.

The gifts continued, every week or so, then every few days. Chocolates, carnations, stuffed animals, scarves, hairbrushes, barrettes, lingerie. Caroline, increasingly anxious, moved in with Dean, and quickly came down with a horrendous cold.

Hourly he would check on her, administering juice, echinacea, or antihistamines, then would go back to the refuge of his workshop. It was where he was most comfortable—alone with his tools and wood, making chairs that would last hundreds of years. He made only armchairs now, one chair, over and over, the Kaneshiro Chair. Each one was fashioned out of a single board of *keyaki,* Japanese zelkova, and was completely handmade. From the logging to the tung oil finish, the wood never touched a power tool. All of Dean's saws and chisels and planes were hand-forged in Japan, and he shunned vises and clamps of any kind, sometimes holding pieces between his feet to work on them.

On first sight, the chair's design wasn't that special— blocky right angles, thick Mission-style slats—but its beauty lay in the craftsmanship. Dean used no nails or screws, no dowels or even glue. Everything was put together by joints, forty-four delicate, intricate joints, modeled after a traditional method of Japanese joinery dating to the seventeenth century, called *sashimono*. Once coupled, the joints were tenaciously, permanently locked. They would never budge, they would never so much as squeak.

What's more, every surface was finished with a hand plane. Dean would not deign to have sandpaper in his shop. He had apprenticed for four years with a master carpenter in the city of Matsumoto, in Nagano prefecture, spending the first six months just learning how to sharpen his tools. When he returned to California, he could pull a block plane over a board and produce a continuous twelve-foot-long shaving, without a single skip or dig, that was less than a tenth of a millimeter thick—so thin you could read a newspaper through it.

Dean aimed for perfection with each chair. With the first kerf of his *dozuki* saw, with the initial chip of a chisel, he was committed to the truth of the cut. Tradition dictated that any errors could not be repaired, but had to remain untouched to remind the woodworker of his humble nature. More and more, Dean liked to challenge himself. He no longer used a level, square, or marking gauge, relying on his eye, and soon he planned to dispense with rulers altogether, maybe even with pencils and chalk. He wanted to get to the point where he could make a Kaneshiro Chair blindfolded.

But he had a problem. Japanese zelkova, the one- to two-thousand-year-old variety he needed, was rare and very expensive—amounting to over $150 a pound. There were only three traditional woodcutters left in Japan, and Dean's sawyer, Hayashi Kota, was sixty-nine. Hayashi-san's intuition was irreplaceable. So much of the work was in reading the trees and determining where to begin sawing to reveal the best figuring and grain—like cutting diamonds. Afraid the sawyer might die soon, Dean had begun stockpiling wood five years ago. In his lumber shed, which was climate-controlled to keep the wood at a steady thirty-seven percent humidity, was about two hundred thousand dollars' worth of zelkova. Hayashi-san cut the logs through and through and air-dried them in Japan for a year, and after two weeks of kiln heat, the boards were shipped to Dean, who stacked them on end in *boule* order. When he went into the shed to select a new board, he was always overcome by the beauty of the wood, the smell of it. He'd run his hand over the boards—hardly a check or crack on them—and would want to weep.

Given the expense of the wood and the precision his chairs required, anyone seeing Dean in his shop would have been shocked by the rapidity with which he worked. He never hesitated. He *attacked* the wood, chips flying, shavings whirling into the air, sawdust piling at his feet. He could sustain this ferocity for hours, never letting his concentration flag. No wonder, then, that it took him a few moments to hear the knocking on the door late that afternoon. It took him even longer to comprehend why anyone would be disturbing him in his workshop, his *sanctum sanctorum*.

Caroline swung open the door and stepped inside, looking none too happy. "You have a visitor," she said.

Marcella Ahn sidled past her. "Hello!"

Dean almost dropped his *ryoba* saw.

"Is that my chair?" she asked, pointing to the stack of two-by-twos on his bench. "I know, I know, you told me not to come, but I had to. You won't hold it against me, will you?"

Without warning, Caroline let out a violent sneeze, her hair whiplashing forward.

"Bless you," Dean and Marcella said at the same time.

Caroline snorted up a long string of snot, glaring at Oriental Hair Poet No. 2. They were a study in contrasts, Marcella once again decked out as an Edwardian whore: a corset and bodice, miniskirt and high heels, full makeup, hair glistening. Caroline was wearing her usual threadbare cardigan and flannel shirt, pajama bottoms, and flip-flops. She hadn't bathed in two days, sick in bed the entire time.

"When you get over this cold," Marcella said to her, "we'll have to get together and catch up. I just can't get over seeing you here."

"It *is* incredible, isn't it?" Caroline said. "It must defy all the laws of probability." She walked to the wall and lifted a mortise chisel from the rack. "The chances of your moving here, when you could live anywhere in the world, it's probably more likely for me to shit an egg for breakfast. Why *did* you move here?"

"Pure chance," Marcella told her cheerily. "I happened to stop for coffee on my way to Aptos, and I saw one of those real estate circulars for this house. It looked like an unbelievable bargain. Beautiful woodwork. I thought, What the hell, I might as well see it while I'm here. I was tired of living in cities."

"What have you been doing since you got to town? Buying lots of gifts?"

Dean watched her dig the chisel blade into a piece of scrap. He wished she would put the chisel down. It was very sharp.

Marcella appeared confused. "Gifts? No. Well, unless you

count Mr. Kaneshiro's chair as a gift. To myself. You don't have a finished one here? I've actually never seen one except in the Museum of Modern Art."

"Sorry," he told her, nervous now, hoping it would slip by Caroline.

But it did not. "The Museum of Modern Art?" she asked. "In New York?"

Marcella nodded. She absently flicked her hair back with her hand, and one of her bracelets flew off her wrist, pinging against the window and landing on some wood chips.

Caroline speared it up with the chisel and dangled it in front of Marcella, who slid it off somewhat apprehensively. Caroline then turned to Dean. "Your chairs are in the Museum of Modern Art in New York?"

He shrugged. "Just one."

"You didn't know?" Marcella asked Caroline, plainly pleased she didn't. "Your boyfriend's quite famous."

"How famous?"

"I would like to get back to work now," Dean said.

"He's in Cooper-Hewitt's permanent collection, the M.F.A. in Boston, the American Craft Museum."

"I need to work, please."

"Don't you have a piece in the White House?"

"Time is late, please."

"Can I ask you some questions about your process?"

"No." He grabbed the chisel out of Caroline's hand before she could react and ushered Marcella Ahn to the door. "Okay, thank you. Goodbye."

"Caroline, when do you want to get together? Maybe for tea?"

"She'll call you," Dean said, blocking her way back inside.

"You'll give her my number?"

"Yes, yes, thank you," he said, and shut the door.

Caroline was sitting on his planing bench, looking gaunt and exhausted. Through the window behind her, Dean saw it was nearing dusk, the wind calming down, the trees quiet. Marcella Ahn was out of view, but he could hear her starting her car, then driving away. He sat down next to Caroline and rubbed her back. "You should go back to bed. Are you hungry? I could make you something."

"Is there anything else about you I should know? Maybe you've taught at Yale or been on the Pulitzer committee? Maybe you've won a few genius grants?"

He wagged his head. "Just one."

"What?"

He told her everything. Earlier in his career, he had done mostly conceptual woodwork, more sculpture than furniture. His father was indeed a fifth-generation Japanese carpenter, as he'd told her, but Dean had broken with tradition, leaving his family's cabinetmaking business in San Luis Obispo to study studio furniture at the Rhode Island School of Design. After graduating, he had moved to New York, where he was quickly declared a phenomenon, a development that baffled him. People talked about his work with terms like "verticality" and "negation of ego" and "primal tension," and they might as well have been speaking Farsi. He rode it for all it was worth, selling pieces at a record clip. But eventually, he became bored. He didn't experience any of the rivalries that Caroline had, nor was he too bothered by the egos and fatuity that abounded in the art world. He just didn't believe in what he was doing anymore, particularly after his father died of a sudden stroke. Dean wanted to return to the pure craftsmanship and functionality of woodworking, building something people could actually *use*. So he dropped everything to apprentice in Japan. Afterward, he distilled all of his knowledge into the Kaneshiro Chair, which was regarded as significant a landmark as Frank Lloyd Wright's Willits Chair. Ironically, his work was celebrated anew. He received a five-year genius grant that paid him an annual $50,000, all of which he had put into hoarding the zelkova in his shed.

"How much do you get a chair?" Caroline asked.

"Ten thousand."

"God, you're only thirty-eight."

"It's an inflated market."

"And you never thought to tell me any of this in the eight months we've been going out? I thought you were barely getting by. You live in this crappy little house with cheap furniture, your pickup is ten years old, you never take vacations. I thought it was because you weren't very savvy about your business, making one chair at a time, no advertising or catalogue or anything, no store lines. I thought you were *clueless*."

"It's not important."

"Not important? Are you insane? Not important? It changes everything."

"Why?"

"You know why, or you wouldn't have kept this secret from me."

"It was an accident. I didn't set out to be famous. It just happened. I'm ashamed of it."

"You should be. You're either pathologically modest, or you were afraid I'd be repelled by how successful you are, compared to me. But you should have told me."

"I just make chairs now," Dean said. "I'm just like you with your poetry. I work hard like you. I don't do it for the money or the fame or to be popular with the critics."

"It's just incidental that you've gotten all of those things without even trying."

"Let's go in the house. I'll make you dinner."

"No. I have to go home. I can't be with you anymore."

"Caroline, please."

"You must think I'm pathetic, you must pity me," she said. "You're not like me at all. You're just like Marcella."

▪   ▪   ▪

THEY had had fights before, puzzling affairs where she would walk out in a huff, incensed by an innocuous remark he'd made, a mysterious gaffe he'd committed. A day or two would go by, then she would talk to him, peevishly at first, ultimately relenting after she had dressed him down with a pointed lecture on his need to be more sensitive, more supportive, more complimentary, more assertive, more emotive, more sympathetic, above all, more *communicative*. Dean would listen without protest, and, newly educated and humbled, he would always be taken back. But not this time. This time was different. On the telephone the next day, Caroline was cool and resolute—no whining or nagging, no histrionics or ultimatums or room for negotiation. "It's over, Dean," she said.

The following afternoon, he went to her apartment with a gallon of *miso* soup. "For your cold," he said.

She looked down at the tub in his hands. "I'm fine now. I don't need the soup. The cold's gone."

They were standing outside on the stairway landing. "You're not going to let me in?" he asked.

"Dean, didn't you hear what I said yesterday?"

"Just tell me how I should change. I'll change."

"It's not like that."

"What's it like, then? Tell me what you want me to do."

"Nothing," she said. "You can't fix this. Don't come by again, don't call, okay? It'll be easier if we just break it off clean."

He tried to leave her alone, but none of it made any sense to him. Why was she ending it? What had he done wrong? It had to be one of her mood swings, a little hormonal blip, a temporary synaptic disruption, all of which he'd witnessed and weathered before. It had to be more about Marcella Ahn than him. She couldn't really be serious. The best course of action seemed to be to wait it out, while at the same time being solicitous and attentive. So he called—not *too* frequently, maybe once a day or so—and since she wouldn't pick up her phone, he left messages: "I just wanted to see how you're doing. I miss you." He drove to her apartment and knocked on her door, and since she wouldn't answer it, he left care packages: macadamia nuts, coffee, cream, filters, toilet paper, sodas, granola bars, springwater, toothpaste—the everyday staples she always forgot to buy.

Five days passed, and she didn't appear to be weakening. A little desperate, he decided to go to Rae's Diner. When Caroline came out of the kitchen and saw him sitting in her station, she didn't seem surprised, but she was angry. She wouldn't acknowledge him, wouldn't come to his table. After twenty minutes, Dean flagged down Rae, the owner. "Could you tell Caroline to take my order?" he asked.

Rae, a lanky, middle-aged brunette with a fierce sunlamp tan, studied him, then Caroline. "If you two are having a fight, I'm not going to be in the middle of it. You want to stay, you'll have to pay."

"That's what I'm trying to do. She won't take my order."

"Why don't you just move to another station?"

"There aren't any other tables."

"The counter, then."

"I'm a paying customer, I should be able to sit where I want."

Rae shook her head. "Any screaming, one little commotion, and you're out of here. And no dawdling over a cup of coffee, either. The minute your table's cleared, you go."

She had a brief conference with Caroline, who began arguing with her, but in the end Rae won out, and Caroline marched over to Dean's table. She didn't look well—pale and baggy-eyed. She wasn't sleeping or eating much, it was clear. He tried to make pleasantries. "How have you been?" he asked her. She would not say a word, much less look at him. She waited for his order, ballpoint poised over her pad. A few minutes later, when his food was ready, she clattered the plate in front of him and walked away. When he raised his coffee cup for a refill, she slopped the pot, spilling coffee over the brim, almost scorching his crotch. He left her a generous tip.

He came to a similar arrangement with the manager of Da Bones, the barbecue restaurant where Caroline worked nights—as long as he paid, he could stay. He ate meals at every one of Caroline's shifts for a week, at the end of which he had gained eight pounds and was popping antacids as if they were gumballs. It was greasy, artery-busting food. A typical breakfast now consisted of six eggs over easy, sausage, hash browns, blueberry flapjacks, coffee, orange juice, biscuits, and milk gravy. Dinner was the hungry man combo—beef brisket, half a rack of baby backs, kielbasa, blackened chicken, rice, beans, slaw, and cornbread—accompanied by a side of mashed and two plates of conch fritters. But it was worth it. Caroline's resolve, he could tell, was beginning to crack (although the same could be said about her health; she looked awful). One night, as he asked for his fifth glass of water, she actually said something. She said, "You are getting to be a real pain in the ass," and she almost smiled. He was getting to her.

But two days later, he received a strange summons. A sergeant from the sheriff's office, Gene Becklund, requested he come down for a talk concerning Caroline. Mystified, Dean drove over to the sheriff's office on Highway 1 and was escorted into an interrogation room. Gene Becklund was a tall, soft-spoken man with prematurely gray hair. He opened the conversation by saying, "You've been going over to your ex-girlfriend's apartment a lot, dropping off little presents? Even though she told you not to call or visit?"

Unsettled, Dean nodded yes.

"You've also been bothering her at her workplace nearly every day?"

"'Bothering'?"

"And you've been leaving a lot of messages on her machine, haven't you?"

"We haven't really broken up," Dean said. "We're just having a fight."

"Uh-huh."

"I'm not harassing her or anything."

"Okay."

"Did she say I was harassing her?"

"Why don't we listen to something," Becklund said, and turned on a cassette player. On the tape was a garbled, robotic, unidentifiable voice, reciting the vile, evil things that would be done to Caroline—anal penetration, disembowelment. "You think you can treat people the way you've treated me, Miss Mighty High?" the voice said. "Think again. I'm going to enjoy watching you die."

"Jesus," Dean said.

Becklund clicked off the tape. "That's just a sample. There have been other calls—very ugly. The voice is disguised. It's hard to even know whether it's a man or a woman."

"The caller used a voice changer."

"You're familiar with them?"

"I read a lot of crime novels."

"I was surprised how cheap the things are. You can get them off the Internet," Becklund said. "The calls were made from various pay phones, mostly between two and four in the morning. Ms. Yip asked the phone company to begin tracing incoming calls a couple of weeks ago. We can trace where they're being made, but not who's making them." Almost as an afterthought, he asked, "You're not making them, are you?"

"No. Is that what Caroline thinks?"

"Here's what I never understand. She *should* think that, everything in my experience says so, but she doesn't. She thinks it's this woman, Marcella Ahn. I've talked to her, too, but she claims she's only left a couple of messages to invite Ms. Yip to tea, and to see if she would do a poetry reading with her at Beryl's Bookstore."

Dean had never really believed it was Marcella Ahn who was leaving the gifts. Maybe an enamored restaurant customer, or the pimply clerk in the hardware store, but not Marcella. Now he reconsidered. "Maybe it's not all a coincidence," he said. "Maybe it is her." Suddenly it almost made sense. "I think it might really be her."

"Maybe," Becklund said. "But my money's on you. Unfortunately, I can't get a restraining order issued without Ms. Yip's cooperation. But I can do this. I can tell you that all the things you did before—the presents, the calls, the workplace visits—weren't prosecutable under the anti-stalking laws until you made a physical threat. You crossed the line with the physical threat. From now on, you make one little slip-up, I can arrest you." He tapped the tabletop with his fingertip. "I suggest you stay away from her."

Dean ignored Becklund. He was frightened for Caroline, and he would do all he could to protect her. The next morning, he waited across the street from the diner for Caroline's shift to finish. When she came outside, he didn't recognize her at first. She had cut off all her hair.

She was walking briskly, carrying a Styrofoam food container, and he had to sprint to catch up to her. "Caroline, please talk to me," he said. "Will you talk to me? Sergeant Becklund told me about the messages."

She stopped but did not turn around. As he stepped in front of her, he saw she was crying. Her hair was shorn to no more than an inch, matted in clumps and tufts, exposing scalp in some places. Evidently she had chopped it off herself in a fit of self-immolation. "Oh, baby," he said, "what have you done?"

She dropped the container, splattering egg salad onto the sidewalk, and collapsed into him. "Do you believe me now?" she asked. "Do you believe it's her?"

"Yes. I do."

"What makes one person want to destroy another?" she asked. "For what? The pettiness, the backstabbing, the meanness—what's the point? Is it fun? She has everything. What more does she want? Why is she doing this to me?"

Dean held her. "I don't know."

"It's such a terrible world, Dean. You can't trust anyone. No matter where you go, there's always someone wishing you ill will. You think they're your friends, and then they're smearing you, trying to ruin you. I can't take this anymore. Why can't she just go away? Can't you make her go away?"

"Is that what you want?"

"Yes," Caroline said.

It was all Dean needed to hear. He took her to his house, put her to bed, and got to work.

▪   ▪   ▪

IT didn't take long to learn her routine. Caroline had been right: Marcella Ahn never left her house until near sunset, when she would go to the newly renovated Y.M.C.A. to attend a cardioboxing class, topped off with half an hour on the StairMaster. She usually didn't shower at the Y, but would go straight home in her workout clothes. At nine or so, she might emerge and drive to Beryl's Bookstore & Café in town for a magazine and a cappuccino. Once, she went to the Moonside Trading Post for a video. Another time, the Safeway on Highway 71 at two A.M. She had one guest, a male, dressed in a suit, an O.B./G.Y.N. at a San Francisco hospital, according to the parking sticker on his BMW. He spent the night. She didn't go anywhere near Caroline's apartment or make any clandestine calls from pay phones.

Dean didn't try to conceal his stakeouts from Caroline, but he misled her into thinking he wanted to catch Marcella in the act. He had no such expectations. By this time, Marcella had to know that she was—however removed—a suspect, that she might be watched. Dean had an entirely different agenda.

One afternoon, he interrupted his surveillance to go to a spy hobbyist shop in San Francisco. He had found it through the Internet on the Rosarita Bay Library computer—Sergeant Becklund had given him the idea. At the store, he bought a lock pick set, $34.95, and a portable voice changer, $29.95. (The clerk also tried to sell him a 200,000-volt stun gun, on sale for $119.95.) Dean paid cash—no credit card records or bank statements to implicate him later.

In the dead of night, he made a call from a pay phone in the neighboring town of Miramar to his own answering machine, imitating the taunts he'd heard in the sheriff's office with the voice changer. "Hey, Jap boyfriend, you're back together with her, are you? Well, fear not, I know where you live." Before leaving the house, he had switched off his telephone's ringer and turned down the volume on the answering machine. He didn't want to scare Caroline, even though she was likely asleep, knocked out by the sleeping pills prescribed by a doctor he'd taken her to see at the town clinic. Still, in the morning, he had no choice but to play the message for her. Otherwise, she wouldn't have called Becklund in a panic, imploring him to arrest Marcella Ahn. "She's insane," Caroline told him. "She's trying to drive me crazy. She's going to try to kill me. You have to do something."

Becklund came to Dean's house, listened to the tape, and appeared to have a change of heart. Dean and Caroline had reconciled. There was no reason to suspect him anymore. Becklund had to look elsewhere. "Keep your doors and windows locked," he told Dean.

After that, the only question was when. It couldn't be too soon, but each day of waiting became more torturous.

The following Wednesday, before her dinner shift, he drove Caroline to Rummy Creek and parked on the headlands overlooking the ocean. It was another miserable, gray, windy day, Dean's truck buffeted by gusts. Rummy Creek was world famous for its big waves, and there was supposed to be a monster swell approaching, but the water was flat, a clump of surfers in the distance bobbing gently on the surface like kelp.

"There haven't been any phone calls all week," Caroline said inside his truck.

"I know. Maybe she's decided to stop."

"No," Caroline said, "she'd never stop. Something's going to happen. I can feel it. I'm scared, Dean."

He dropped her off at Da Bones, then drove up Skyview Ridge Road and nestled in the woods outside Marcella's house. On schedule, she left for the Y.M.C.A. at six P.M. After a few minutes, he strolled to the door as casually as possible. She didn't have a neighbor within a quarter mile, but he worried about the unforeseen—the gynecologist lover, a UPS delivery, Becklund deciding belatedly to serve a restraining order. Wearing latex surgical gloves, Dean inserted a lock pick and tension bar into the keyhole on the front door. The deadbolt opened within twenty seconds. Thankfully she had not installed an alarm system yet. He took off his shoes and walked through the kitchen into the garage. This was the biggest variable in his plan. If he didn't find what he needed there, none of it would work. But to his relief, Marcella Ahn had several cans of motor oil on the shelf, as well as some barbecue lighter fluid—it wasn't gasoline, but it would do. In the recycle bin, there were four empty bottles of pinot grigio. In the kitchen, a funnel and a dishrag. He poured one part motor oil and one part lighter fluid into a bottle, a Molotov cocktail recipe provided by the Internet. In her bedroom, he pulled several strands of hair from her brush, pocketed one of her bracelets, and grabbed a pair of platform-heeled boots from her closet. Then he was out, and he sped to his house in Vasquez Canyon. All he had to do was press in some boot-prints in the dirt in front of the lumber shed, but he was running out of time. He drove back to Marcella's, hurriedly washed the soles of the boots in the kitchen sink, careful to leave a little mud, replaced the boots in the closet, checked through the house, and locked up. Then he went to Santa Cruz and tossed the lock pick set and voice changer into a dumpster.

He did nothing more until three A.M. By then, Caroline was unconscious from the sleeping pills. Dean drove to Marcella

Ahn's again. He had to make sure she was home, and alone. He walked around her house, peeking into the windows. She was in her study, sitting at her desk in front of her laptop computer. She had her head in her hands, and she seemed to be quietly weeping. Dean was overcome with misgivings for a moment. He had to remind himself that she was at fault here, that she deserved what was coming to her.

He returned to his own property. Barefoot and wearing only the latex gloves and his underwear, he snagged the strands of Marcella's hair along the doorframe of the lumber shed. He threw the bracelet toward the driveway. He twisted the dishrag into the mouth of the wine bottle, then tilted it from side to side to mix the fluids and soak the rag. He started to flick his lighter, but then hesitated, once more stalled by doubt. Were those mystery novels he read really that accurate? Would the Hair & Fiber and Latent Prints teams be deceived at all? Was he being a fool—a complete amateur who would be ferreted out with ease? He didn't know. All he knew was that he loved Caroline, and he had to take this risk for her. If something wasn't done, he was certain he would lose her. He lit the rag and smashed the bottle against the first stack of zelkova inside the shed. The fire exploded up the boards. He shut the door and ran back into the house and climbed into bed beside Caroline. In a matter of seconds, the smoke detectors went off. The shed was wired to the house, and the alarm in the hallway rang loud enough to wake Caroline. "What's going on?" she asked.

Dean peered out the window. "I think there's a fire," he said. He pulled on his pants and shoes and ran to the shed. When he kicked open the door, the heat blew him back.

Flames had already engulfed three *boules* of wood, the smoke was thick and black, the fire was spreading. Something had gone wrong. The sprinkler system—his expensive, state-of-the-art, dry-pipe sprinkler system—had not activated. He had not planned to sacrifice this much wood, one or two stacks at most, and now he was in danger of losing the entire shed.

■　　　■　　　■

THERE was no investigation, per se. Two deputies took photographs and checked for fingerprints, but that was about all. Dean asked Becklund, "Aren't you going to call the crime lab unit?" and Becklund said, "This is it."

It was simple enough for the fire department to determine that it was arson, but not who set it. The insurance claims adjuster was equally lackadaisical. Within a few days, he signed off for Dean to receive a $75,000 check. Dean and Caroline had kept the blaze contained with extinguishers and garden hoses for the twenty-two minutes it took for the fire trucks to arrive, but nearly half of Dean's wood supply had been consumed, the rest damaged by smoke and water.

No charges were filed against Marcella Ahn. After talking to Becklund and a San Vicente County assistant district attorney, though, she agreed—on the advice of counsel—to move out of Rosarita Bay, which was hardly a great inconvenience for her, since she owned five other houses and condos. Caroline never heard from her again, and, as far as they knew, she never published another book—a one-hit wonder.

Caroline, on the other hand, finally submitted her second book to a publisher. Dean was relentless about making her do so. The book was accepted right away, and when it came out, it caused a brief sensation. Great reviews. Awards and fellowships. Dozens of requests for readings and appearances. Caroline couldn't be bothered. By then, she and Dean had had their first baby, a girl, Anna, and Caroline wanted more children, a baker's dozen if possible. She was transformed. No more nightmares, and she could nap standing up (housekeeping remained elusive). In relation to motherhood, to the larger joys and tragedies that befell people, the poetry world suddenly seemed silly, insignificant. She would continue to write, but only, she said, when she had the time and will. Of course, she ended up producing more than ever.

Marcella Ahn's chair was the last Dean made from the pristine zelkova. He would dry and clean up the boards that were salvageable, and when he exhausted that supply, he would switch to English walnut, a nice wood—pretty, durable, available.

He delivered the chair to Marcella just before she left town, on May 11, as scheduled. She was surprised to see him and the chair, but a promise was a promise. He had never failed to deliver an order, and she had prepaid for half of it.

He set the chair down in the living room—crowded with boxes and crates—and she sat in it. "My God," she said, "I didn't know it would be this comfortable. I could sit here all day."

"I'd like to ask you for a favor," Dean said as she wrote out a check for him. He held an envelope in his hand.

"A favor?"

"Yes. I'd like you to read Caroline's new poems and tell me if they're good."

"You must be joking. After everything she's done?"

"I don't know poetry. You're the only one who can tell me. I need to know."

"Do you realize I could have been sent to state prison for two years? For a crime I didn't commit?"

"It would've never gone to trial. You would've gotten a plea bargain—a suspended sentence and probation."

"How do you know?" Marcella asked. "Your girlfriend is seriously deranged. I only wanted to be her friend, and she devised this insidious plot to frame me and run me out of town. She's diabolical."

"You stalked her."

"I did no such thing. Don't you get it? She faked it. She set me up. *She* was the stalker. Hasn't that occurred to you? Hasn't that gotten through that thick, dim-witted skull of yours? She burned your *wood*."

"You're lying. You're very clever, but I don't believe you," Dean said. And he didn't, although she made him think for a second. He pulled out the book manuscript from the envelope. "Are you going to read the poems or not?"

"No."

"Aren't you curious what she's been doing for the past six years?" Dean asked. "Isn't this what you came here to find out?"

Marcella slowly hooked her hair behind her ears and took her time to respond. "Give it to me," she finally said.

For the next half hour, she sat in his chair in the living room, flipping through the seventy-one pages, and Dean watched her. Her expression was unyielding and contemptuous at first, then it went utterly slack, then taut again. She breathed quickly through her nose, her jaw clamped, her eyes blinked.

"Are they good?" Dean asked when she finished.

She handed the manuscript back to him. "They're pedestrian. They're clunky. There's no music to the language."

"They're good," Dean told her.

"I didn't say that."

"You don't have to. I saw it in your face." He walked to the door and let himself out.

"I didn't say they were good!" Marcella Ahn screamed after him. "Do you hear me? I didn't say that. I didn't say they were good!"

Dean never told Caroline about his last visit with Marcella Ahn, nor did he ever ask her about the stalking, although he was tempted at times. One spring afternoon, they were outside on his deck, Caroline leaning back in the rocker he'd made for her, her eyes closed to the sun, Anna asleep in her lap. It had rained heavily that winter, and the eucalyptus and pine surrounding the house were now in full leaf. They sat silently and listened to the wind bending through the trees. He had rarely seen her so relaxed.

Anna, still asleep, lolled her head, her lips pecking the air in steady rhythm—an infant soliloquy.

"Caroline," he said.

"Hm?"

"What do you think she's dreaming about?"

Caroline looked down at Anna. "Your guess is as good as mine," she said. "Maybe she has a secret. Can babies have secrets?" She ran her hand through her hair, which she had kept short, and she smiled at Dean.

Was it possible that Caroline had fabricated everything about Marcella Ahn? He did not want to know. She would, in turn, never question him about the fire. The truth wouldn't have mattered. They had each done what was necessary to be with the other. Such was the price of love among artists, such was the price of devotion.

VOIR DIRE

ON SUNDAY afternoon, when Hank Low Kwon returned to his house in Rosarita Bay, he found a note tacked to his front door. "You don't think I *read*?" it said. The note was unsigned, but he knew it was from Molly Beddle. No doubt she had seen the newspaper article, small as it was, summarizing the first day of the trial, and was miffed that he had mentioned it only tangentially to her. It was clearly his biggest case in four years as a public defender.

He had been working at his San Vicente office all day and didn't know where Molly would be. He tried her at her loft, at the sports center and gym, and then, on a hunch, dialed the marine forecast—northwest at twenty-three knots, gusting to thirty—and was certain he would find her at Rummy Creek, her favorite windsurfing spot.

From Highway 1, he turned onto a dirt fire road that cut through a barbed-wire fence with no trespassing signs, bumped down half a mile of scrub grass, wound past the Air Force radar station, and then arrived at the headlands bordering the ocean. Molly's truck was there, parked among a handful of cars, and Hank stepped to the edge of the cliff to look for her.

It didn't take long. She was flying across the water, feet in the board's straps, hooked to the boom in her harness, raking the sail back so far, she was almost lying flat—a human catamaran. She carved the board into a sweeping turn, executing a smooth laydown jibe, and raced back to shore. She jibed again, accelerated toward a small wave, and launched off its lip, swooping fifteen feet into the air, and then touched down without missing a beat.

Hank sat on a tree stump and watched her. Molly had once described the feeling she got out there, sometimes flailing, struggling just to keep her balance and hang on to the boom, and then getting into a slot where everything fell into place, hydroplaning on the tail of the board, lightly skimming over the chop. At that moment, going as fast as she could, it was effortless. She could take one hand off the rig, let her fingers drag in the water. She could look around, catch a little scenery—the cypress and pine atop the bluffs, the kelp waving underneath the surface. It was glorious, she had said, and, as Molly, finished for the day, waded to the sand, as Hank climbed down the cliff to meet her, he could see the quiet elation in her face, the contentment of a woman who knew what she loved in this world.

But then she spotted Hank. She dropped her board and sail

and marched toward him, sleek and divine in her sleeveless wetsuit. Without a word, she punched her fist into his arm, stinging him so hard with surprise, he fell to the ground. He looked up at her, half laughing. "I can't believe you did that," he said.

"Did it hurt?"

"Yes, it hurt. Like a son of a bitch."

"Good. I feel better now," she said, and helped him to his feet.

THE indictment was on two counts: Penal Code Section 187, second-degree murder, punishable by fifteen years to life, and Section 273a, Subdivision (1), felony child abuse, punishable by one to ten. The previous summer, Chee Seng Lam, a cocaine addict, had beaten his girlfriend's three-year-old son, Simon Liu, to death with an electrical cord, whipping the boy, according to the medical examiner, more than four hundred times.

On Friday at San Vicente Superior Court, before the weekend recess, Hank had given his opening statement. He had told the jury that Lam was not a child abuser; he had never intended to harm Simon Liu that night. Indeed, he hadn't even known it was Simon he was hitting. High on cocaine, hallucinating wildly, he had believed he was lashing at—trying to protect himself from—a nest of snakes, thousands of them.

Drugs alone could not eliminate culpability. To win an acquittal, Hank would have to prove that the coke had made Lam delusional and paranoid, even when he wasn't under the influence—in other words, that he had developed a latent mental defect—and because of it, he was incapable of knowing or understanding the nature and quality of his act, or of distinguishing right from wrong—the legal definition of insanity in California.

"You believe him?" Molly asked as she hosed the salt off her gear in his driveway.

"I don't know," Hank said. "I'm not sure he's smart enough to have made it up."

"Does he have a history of violence?"

"Not against the kid, but yeah, he was your basic piece of shit." Chee Seng Lam had twenty-two prior arrests, mostly as a juvenile, when he had been a member of the Flying Dragons gang: aggravated assault, extortion, burglary, receiving stolen property, gun and drug possession, a couple of other assorted goodies, none of which would ever be revealed in court, since Hank had gotten his record suppressed.

"I guess you won't have too many character witnesses," Molly said.

"His dealer liked him."

Molly restrapped her shortboards on the rack of her truck. She had been a ten-meter platform diver in college, but she was in better shape now, at thirty-five, than she had been at her competitive peak, although most people never suspected it. Largely, this had to do with how little she cared about her looks. She had a sweet, guileless face—eyes set wide apart, a plump mouth, long, wispy blond hair—yet she never wore makeup, and her skin was always sunburned in patches, bruised, scratched, her lips chapped. In the rumpled sweaters and khakis she preferred, she was deceptively ordinary. Solid and thick-boned, one would think; maybe even a little over-weight.

But of course, underneath the baggy attire, it was all muscle and power. Besides windsurfing, Molly skied, kayaked, rock climbed, and occasionally entered a triathlon for fun. She had degrees in biomechanics and sports science, and she was now the head diving coach at San Vicente University, where she had put together a championship program.

Her energy and fitness both attracted and overwhelmed Hank, who'd become, in his late thirties, a bit paunchy and prone to bronchitis. Yet, for all their differences, they got on remarkably well. They had met at the grand opening of Banzai Pipeline, the Japanese restaurant on Main Street. Hank had grown up in Hawaii with the owner, Duncan Roh, a surfer Molly knew from Rummy Creek.

They had been seeing each other for a year and a half now, and recently they had agreed that they would move in together at the end of the summer, when their current leases expired. Both divorced, they were careful not to attach undue significance to the decision. They knew enough not to ask the other for compromise, not to be too preoccupied about defining a future, which had become difficult of late, since Molly was now ten weeks pregnant.

She adjusted the nozzle on the garden hose and took a sip of water. "Would you mind if I came to the trial?" she asked.

"Why would you want to?"

"I want to see you at work. I've never been to a trial."

"You might make me more nervous than I already am," he told her. This was partially true. Out of the two-hundred-fifty-some cases he had handled, only twenty had gone to a jury—a routine track record in the public defenders' office, where the motto was plead 'em and speed 'em.

"Your ex-wife never went to court?"

"Didn't care for the clientele."

Molly pulled her T-shirt over her head.

"What are you doing?" Hank said. He rented a mildewy two-bedroom cottage near Rummy Creek, and his neighbors were out and about.

Molly bent over and sprayed water on her hair, then squeezed it into a ponytail.

Hank noticed a cut on her bicep. "You're bleeding," he told her. He didn't think she should have been windsurfing at all, but pregnancy hadn't slowed her down a bit—no morning sickness, no fatigue.

Molly examined the gash on her arm, then licked the blood and kissed him. "Have you been smoking today?" she asked. "You taste like smoke."

"That's what I like about you. You don't nag. Why don't you put your shirt back on before someone gets a cheap thrill."

She looked down at her breasts. "Amazing. I actually have tits now," she said. "They're so swollen. Feel them."

"Are they tender?"

"A little. You don't want to feel them?"

He handed back her T-shirt. "You really want to come to the trial?"

"Would it disturb you that much?"

"I guess not," he told her. "But it'll be embarrassing to watch."

"Why? Is your case that weak?"

"No, you don't get it," he said. "I think I'm going to win."

LAST summer, on June 23, Ruby Liu drove down from Oakland to San Vicente with her son. She had been looking forward to spending the weekend with Chee Seng Lam, but right away they argued. Lam was irritated she'd brought Simon. "He say Simon noisy," she testified. "He say Simon need discipline."

Later, she and Simon fell asleep in the bedroom while Lam stayed up in the living room, listening to music on his headphones. At approximately one A.M., Ruby awoke and saw that Simon was no longer at her side. She walked down the hall and discovered Lam whipping her son with the cord to his headphones. She pushed Lam away. Simon was moaning, his eyes fluttering, and then he stopped breathing. She called 911. By the time the E.M.T.s arrived, Simon was dead.

From the standpoint of the law, Ruby's testimony was devastating, but she wasn't entirely effective as a witness. She spoke in a rehearsed monotone, eyes down, body impassive and contained, and it was hard to fathom a mother not betraying a single hint of emotion as she related the death of her only child. She seemed to be hiding something. She seemed to be lying.

What everyone but the jury knew was that Ruby Liu was a prostitute and a junkie. She mainlined speedballs—a combination of heroin and cocaine—and she had gone to Lam's apartment that weekend to get high with him. She could have easily been indicted on a slew of negligence charges, so it was no surprise that she had agreed to testify for the prosecution.

"Did Mr. Lam ever hit Simon before?" Hank asked her.

Ruby glanced at the assistant district attorney, John Boudreau, then said no.

"Not once? Maybe an isolated spanking?"

"No."

"So he never hit Simon, or spanked him, or slapped him. Not once. He never even raised his voice to him, did he?"

"He say Simon noisy. He say he need discipline."

"You keep repeating that. Did he say this to you in English or Chinese?"

Ruby blinked several times, trying to choose. "English," she declared.

"How good would you say Mr. Lam's English is?"

"He speak English."

"Is he fluent, or is his English somewhat broken, like yours?"

"Same as me, maybe."

"Can he read and write?"

"Not good."

"Have you ever heard him use the word 'discipline' before?"

She squirmed. "No."

"Are you sure he said 'discipline,' or did someone suggest the word to you?"

"Objection," Boudreau said.

For the next two hours, Hank had Ruby describe Lam's escalating drug use over the five years she'd known him, how eventually he would freebase cocaine for up to twenty hours at a time, sometimes going six days without sleep, obsessed with getting and smoking the coke, ignoring all else.

Increasingly, his behavior became more erratic. He saw bugs, tadpoles. On his body, coming out of his skin, on other people. Without warning, he would slap and scratch himself, claw his fingernails into his arms until he bled. Then he began seeing snakes. Diamondbacks, corals, water moccasins, copperheads, black mambas, cobras, tree vipers—he identified fourteen varieties from library books Ruby stole for him. Lam weather-stripped his doors and sealed every window, covered the heating vents with screens. He would often drop to all fours with a flashlight and a propane torch, hunting for the snakes, burning the floor and furniture.

Once, he beat a sofa cushion with a stick, trying to kill the baby cottonmouths he said were slithering out of it, rending the cushion apart for an hour and a half without pause. He heard voices, he saw ghosts. He thought the government was dumping the snakes into his apartment to kill him, and he drilled peepholes in the walls, bolted a security camera above his front door, and installed listening devices in nearly every room. He would not leave his apartment. Repeatedly, Ruby tried to convince him that the cocaine was making him hallucinate, but he refused to believe her. She was crazy, he said.

"Was he freebasing cocaine the night Simon was killed?"

"Yes."

"When you discovered him standing over Simon in the living room, did you yell at him to stop?"

"Yes."

"And did he respond to you in any way?"

"No."

"So he appeared to be in a trance?" Hank asked.

Ruby frowned. "I don't know," she said. "No."

"Like the time with the sofa cushion?"

"Objection," Boudreau said. "Asked and answered."

Hank withdrew the question and said instead, "Where were the headphones?"

"What?"

"He was holding the cord to his headphones, but where were the headphones themselves?"

"I don't know. His neck, maybe."

"Mr. Lam often spent all night doing cocaine while he listened to music on the headphones?"

"Yes."

"Would you say, then, that when Simon walked in, Mr. Lam must have jumped up in a panic, thinking these snakes—"

Boudreau cut him off. "Calls for speculation, Your Honor," he complained, his face flushing. Boudreau had some form of psoriasis, and whenever he was nervous or rattled—which was all the time—his skin bloomed red. Boudreau asked only one question in his redirect: "Did you ever see Mr. Lam selling drugs?"

"Yeah, he sell drugs."

Hank stood up. "Did he sell drugs to make a profit," he asked, "or just to support his own habit?"

Ruby looked dumbly at Hank. She was exhausted. "Habit, okay?" she said.

After a lengthy sidebar at Hank's request, the judge, Eduardo Gutierrez, instructed the jury that the issue of selling drugs was pertinent only to the defendant's state of mind, not his character. "The fact that Mr. Lam might have sold drugs does not prove he has an inherent disposition to engage in criminal conduct," Gutierrez said, remarkably deadpan.

LAM wore a striped button-down shirt, which was one size too large for him, a tie, and pleated pants—nothing too fancy, but neat. His hair was cut above the ears, and he was clean-shaven. Since he was small and thin to begin with, he looked, by design, harmless—a far cry from the ponytailed, hollow-eyed menace to society Hank had met nine months earlier, when Lam had been released from Cabrillo State Hospital.

In a conference room next to the holding pen, Hank gave Lam a cigarette. Smoking wasn't permitted anymore, but everyone ignored the rule. "You do good," Lam said. "Better than I think."

"I covered all the necessary points."

"No, really. Before, I think you *stupid*."

Hank was used to this reaction. No one had any respect for public defenders—not judges, prosecutors, cops, not the public, least of all clients. "Don't get too smug," he said. "We've got a long way to go."

Lam blew on the tip of his cigarette, reddening the cherry. "Blondie your girlfriend?" Lam said. He'd seen Molly with Hank during a recess. "*Low faan* girlfriend, huh? No like Chinese girls?"

Hank flipped through the pages of his notepad. Like everyone, Lam assumed that Hank was Chinese. He had a Chinese-sounding name, but he was actually Korean, born and raised in Haleiwa, on the North Shore of Oahu, where his father was a Presbyterian minister.

Lam helped himself to another cigarette. As he was lighting it, Hank noticed his eyes—glazed and dilated. "You're stoned," he said.

"Naw."

"Bullshit."

"Just a little pot."

"You idiot. I told you to stay clean."

"You see Ruby? I betcha Valium," Lam said. "Good thing I never marry her. She lie first, you know. Say Simon my baby. But I know. I slap her. My baby? *My* baby? She cry. Boo hoo. Mistake. Big mistake. I'm not *stupid*. Right, Hankie?"

Hank looked at Lam, who was grinning, clowning. "When we get back in the courtroom," he told him, "you don't smile, you don't laugh. You don't act bored or slouch in your chair. Look serious and remorseful. Look like you feel bad about what you've done."

▪   ▪   ▪

THEY were stuck in traffic on Highway 71, coming over the hill from San Vicente to Rosarita Bay. During rush hour, it sometimes took two hours to travel the fifteen miles home.

"I don't think I can make it to the rest of the trial," Molly said.

"No?" Hank asked. She had only attended two days.

"I've got too much work to do."

This was an equivocation, Hank knew, but he was relieved nonetheless.

"Do you think they assigned this case to you because you're Asian?" Molly asked.

"That's rhetorical, right?"

"Because they thought it'd help with the jury?"

"Partly them, mostly the client."

Molly tugged on her seat belt strap, pulling it away from her chest. "You ever wonder what makes people go in one direction and not another?"

"What do you mean?"

"All the little things that add up. I was thinking about Lam and his girlfriend, the model minorities they turned out to be. Aren't you curious about that?"

"I used to be. Not anymore."

"Why not?"

Hank shifted into neutral; they weren't going anywhere. "There's this strangely poetic phrase in the California Penal Code. Malice can be implied if circumstances show 'an abandoned and malignant heart.' Day in and day out, that's what I see. Some people are just evil."

"That's a charitable view of the world. I thought you were such a liberal."

"Given enough time, we all become Republicans."

Before moving to Rosarita Bay, Hank had spent ten years working for a small, progressive law firm in San Francisco, specializing in immigration cases and bias suits. He had always been a true believer—a "left-wing, bleeding-heart pagoda of virtue," his ex-wife, Allison Pak, used to say. He hadn't known what he was getting into four years ago, becoming a public defender. He had been fired up about the presumption of innocence and due process, about the racial

inequities of the judicial system. Now he represented mug-
gers, drug dealers, wife beaters, carjackers, arsonists, thieves,
rapists, and child molesters. They were almost always guilty,
they were all junkies, and if by some technicality Hank was
able to get them off, they'd go right out and do the same
thing, or worse.

He told Molly about one of his first cases in Juvenile
Court, a ten-year-old San Vicente kid who, as he was riding
down the street on his BMX bicycle, swung a pipe into a
man's face. No reason. Didn't know him, didn't rob him. Just
felt like it. Hank found out some things about the kid's back-
ground—broken home, physical abuse—and thought he
deserved another chance. A month later, the kid participated
in a home invasion. He raped and sodomized a six-year-old
girl with a broomstick, a beer bottle, and a light bulb, which
he busted inside her, and then, for good measure, hammered
a few nails into her heels.

"You're having a crisis of faith," Molly said.

"Is it that obvious?"

"It's just this case. You'll get over it."

"You're horrified by it. How can you not be? I'm defend-
ing a baby-killer."

They finally crossed Skyview Ridge and headed downhill
to Rosarita Bay. Hank rolled down the window and breathed
in the chaparral and the ocean. Rosarita Bay was part of San
Vicente County, but this side of the peninsula mountains, the
Coastside, was a remote outpost in the tundra compared to
the industrial Bayside city of San Vicente. To Hank, it was
well worth the commute to be out of the fray.

They stopped by Hank's cottage to pick up one of his suits,

then went to Molly's loft, which was in a converted cannery next to the harbor. Once inside, Molly said, "I have to pee. It's incredible how many times I have to pee these days."

There was a mini-trampoline on the floor, near the foot of her bed, and on the way to the bathroom, Molly nonchalantly hopped onto it and did a forward flip. She grinned back mischievously at Hank.

For a while, the trampoline had been an instrument of ritual. Whenever Molly wanted to make love, she would bounce off the tramp, tumble through the air, and flop onto the bed. "Time to make Molly jolly," she'd say. Sometimes, growling: "Tiger Lily want her Moo Shi Kwon."

At first, Molly's sexual assertion had unnerved him. When they began dating, she had been subdued and uncomfortable, and he had been certain, each time he called her, that she would not see him again. At the end of their fourth date— another disaster, he had thought—he drove her home and lightly kissed her cheek goodnight. She stayed in the car, cracking her knuckles. "That's *it*?" she suddenly blurted. "You mean you're *done* with me?" Then she had ravished him, taking him inside to the loft and stripping him of his clothes.

With Molly, all roads originated in the body. Her entire life, she had spoken through it—joy found in challenging limits and conquering the elements, being fearless, perfect, indomitable. There were no moral ambiguities in her life. What she did was pure.

When she came out of the bathroom, she joined Hank on the couch, and he massaged her feet, kneading his thumbs into her instep.

"Hank," she said, "why don't you want this baby?"

When she had first revealed she was pregnant, he had told her he would support her either way, but it was her decision to make. He wouldn't say it explicitly, but it was clear he favored an abortion. "I just wish it was something we'd planned," he said to her now.

"Is it because I'm not Korean?"

"God, no," Hank said. "Where'd that come from?"

She wiggled her toes, signaling for him to switch feet. "I think I saw your ex-wife today."

"What?"

"At the courthouse. One floor up. The bathroom across the hall was being cleaned, so I went upstairs."

"Are you sure it was her?" Hank asked. Molly had seen photographs of Allison, but had never met her.

Molly nodded. "She's very pretty."

░   ░   ░

THE photographs hurt. There were five of them—all color eight-by-tens—and they sat on Boudreau's table for the next two days as he called up the firemen who were first on the scene, the E.M.T.s who tried to revive Simon, and the police officers who arrested Lam. With each witness, Boudreau brought out the photographs and asked, "Do they accurately and fairly depict the condition of the boy as you found him?" And each of these grown men, these veterans of daily, horrific violence, would wince looking at the pictures, then choke out yes.

Each of them confirmed that Lam had pointed to the head-phone cord when questioned what he beat Simon with, that he had kept repeating he wasn't a child beater, and that though he seemed agitated, he was coherent, even asking to change his clothes and put on his shoes before being cuffed. He did not mention any hallucinations. Not a word about snakes.

The county medical examiner testified that he had counted 417 separate and distinct contusions and abrasions, and the cord was consistent with the injuries. At some point, he said, the cord must have been doubled up, which would explain some of the U-shaped marks. The official cause of death was swelling and bleeding of the brain caused by trauma, which forced the brain into its base and cut off breathing functions.

"You also found a large lump on the back of his head?" Hank asked.

"A blunt force injury on the occipital lobe."

"Was it caused by the cord?"

"No. Most likely he fell backwards to the floor and hit his head."

"He tripped and fell down."

"Or he was pushed."

"Could the fall have rendered Simon unconscious the whole time?"

"That's impossible to determine."

"Is it *possible,* however?"

"I suppose."

"Could the fall, bumping his head, have been the actual cause of death?"

The M.E., seeing where Hank was going, smirked and said, "Unlikely."

"But it's possible?"

Boudreau objected, and Gutierrez had them approach. "You know better than to challenge proximate cause," he told Hank. "Move it along."

Hank held up the plastic evidence bag containing the headphones. "It's been stipulated that this cord is ten feet long, but only one-sixteenth of an inch wide. *With* the headphones, it weighs less than three ounces. Wouldn't you say it's pretty ineffective as a weapon?"

"It seemed to do the trick."

"But considering how light it is, it's rather awkward to use as a whip, isn't it? Even doubled up?"

"I wouldn't know."

"Did the injuries indicate a repetitive motor motion?"

"Obviously."

"The same action, over and over, like a mindless robot?"

"I can't make that characterization."

"But you *are* an expert on injuries resulting from the application of specific weapons?"

"I am that."

Hank showed the M.E. two photographs of Lam's living room and passed copies to the jurors, which was decidedly risky, since they would spot the V.C.R.s stacked in Lam's apartment and might surmise, correctly, that he had been fencing them. "If Mr. Lam really wanted to inflict pain, 'discipline' someone, as it were, wouldn't the baseball bat—right here in the photograph, right next to where they found the deceased—wouldn't it have been more effective?"

"That depends," the M.E. said.

"What about this broomstick here? Or this belt?"

The M.E. sighed. "Mr. Kwon, a piece of dental floss, tight-

ened around a tender part of the body, could be more excruciating than many more obvious methods of torture. Its general
innocuousness as an implement of hygiene does not remove its
lethal potential. What happened to this boy was brutal, and it
caused him unimaginable pain, and it killed him."

▪   ▪   ▪

"MAYBE wrong before," Lam said in the conference room.
"Maybe you really stupid."

Hank lit a cigarette. Lam, wanting one, motioned to Hank,
who ignored him.

"Hey," Lam said. "C'mon."

Hank forcefully slid the pack across the table, bouncing it
off Lam's chest.

Lam tsked. "Be nice."

"Tell me something," Hank said. "How do you know
Simon wasn't your kid?"

"Huh?"

"What makes you so sure he wasn't your son?"

"You crazy? Ruby whore. She slam heroin with needle.
Always use condom. No want AIDS, you know."

"You had no feelings for him?"

Lam shrugged. "Make noise. Run run. Break stereo.
Always cry. No food. No toy. Little whore baby. Ruby no
care. You think Simon become doctor? Maybe lawyer, like
you? Better dead."

In the medical examiner's photographs, Simon's entire
body—all two feet, thirty pounds of him—had been covered
with welts and bruises and cuts, only the palms of his hands
and the soles of his feet spared.

Hank watched Lam brush a stray cigarette ash from his shirtsleeve.

A few days ago, Hank had found a pregnancy book in Molly's loft, hidden in a cupboard. He had read a passage in the book that she had underlined. At twelve weeks, the fetus would be fully formed. It would have eyelids, thirty-two tooth buds, finger- and toenails. It would be able to swallow, press its lips together, frown, clench its fists. It would be, at that point, two and a half inches long.

"It sickens me to think I might let you walk," he told Lam.

"Too bad. You have job."

"I find myself asking what would happen if I slipped a little, made a mistake here and there."

"No choice. You have job. You do best."

"Maybe I already fucked up on purpose. You were right about the medical examiner. I'm usually smarter than that."

"No, you too much goodie-goodie. You never do that."

"No?"

"Naw."

"The funny thing is, you wouldn't be able to tell. No one would. If I'm not blatantly incompetent, no one would ever know."

Lam giggled, then slowly quieted down, growing uncertain. "Better not," he said. "Better not, you fuck."

"Who would it hurt?"

▫   ▫   ▫

THEY got their drinks at the bar and snagged a table near the front window. The restaurant was crowded—a popular hangout for those who worked at the courthouse.

"This place is a pit," Allison said.

"There's not much else around here," Hank said.

"I hate San Vicente."

Hank had checked the dockets and had found his ex-wife upstairs, representing a consulting firm that was being sued for breach of contract.

"The details would put you to sleep," she told Hank. She was still hoping to settle.

They caught up a little. It had been about a year since they'd run into each other. Allison looked good, crisp in her starched white blouse and silk suit. Her hair was longer, chin-length now, parted in the middle and tucked behind her ears. She'd had a short blunt cut before, which had pronounced her sucked-in cheeks and skinny frame, making her seem even more acerbic and severe than she was.

They had been divorced for three years, almost as long as they had been married. They had been mismatched from the beginning, always getting into fights about politics and money ("kuppie," he would call her—Korean yuppie), trading indictments about his moronic crusades and her nauseating self-absorption, epitomized, he felt, by her refusal to have children. They had mistaken their hostility for passion and stayed together longer than they should have.

She was now living in San Francisco with a wealthy developer named Jason Chu, an A.B.C., American-born Chinese, who, coincidentally, had been trying for the last decade to build a $50 million monstrosity in Rosarita Bay: two hundred houses around a golf course, a shopping mall, a hotel and conference center, and a fake lighthouse.

"Is he still trying to get that passed?" Hank asked. "He'll never get it to fly. Not in Rosarita Bay."

"How can you live there?"

"It's nice."

"It's hicksville. You might as well be in the Farm Belt," Allison told him. "Jason says it's racism, the reason why he can't get zoning. In your former life, he might've been a client of yours. Get this. I read him the article about your trial, your lovely Mr. Lam, and Jason said, 'That can't be right. Chinese don't do drugs.'"

"Ha."

"How's your diver friend? Martha?"

"Molly. Don't try to be cute. You know her name."

"So, how are things going?"

"She's pregnant."

"*Well*," Allison said expansively. "Congratulations. You're finally going to be a pa*pa*."

"Maybe not," Hank said.

"What do you mean? You knocked her up by *accident*?"

"I don't know how it happened."

"I'm guessing it was a Freudian spurt. It's what you've always wanted, isn't it? Do you love her?"

Hank lit a cigarette.

"I thought you quit," Allison said.

"I did."

"Well, do you? Love her?"

Hank nodded.

"Enough to marry her one of these days?"

He nodded again.

"What gives, then?"

Hank tried to flag down the waitress for another drink, but she didn't notice him. He hesitated, then asked Allison, "Why didn't you want a child with me?"

"I thought it was because I'm a selfish bitch. Because I'm—"

"Don't start."

"I always hated that about you. Your moral superiority. What made you think you were so much better than everyone else? Now look at you, with this scumbag Lam. That'd be quite a precedent if you win. Negate culpability for anyone on drugs. Some way to save the world."

"Do we have to do this?"

"No, I suppose not," Allison said. "But you could've let me enjoy myself a bit longer." She reapplied lipstick to her mouth.

Hank fiddled with his empty drink glass. "Did you think I wouldn't be a good father?"

She turned to him. "No, I never thought that," she said, softening. "What's going on with you? What are you afraid of?"

"These days, everything."

"I don't like seeing you like this. It's fun beating you up once in a while, but only if you fight back."

"Ironic, isn't it?" Hank said. "I used to think not wanting a child was selfish. Now I think wanting one is."

▪   ▪   ▪

His defense took four days. He had a narcotics detective testify that, contrary to Boudreau's suggestions, Lam was not a dealer of any consequence. The paraphernalia found in his apartment was used for freebasing, a somewhat antiquated method of smoking coke, reserved for connoisseurs and hard-core addicts. Instead of heating cocaine hydrochloride powder with baking soda, which would yield crack, Lam separated the base with ether and a propane torch. Freebase was purer than crack, but no dealer today went through the trouble of producing it. It took too long, and it was dangerous. And although crack houses had precision scales and surveillance equipment like Lam's, most dealers did not have any reason to monitor the *inside* of the house. There was also no currency found in the apartment, no vials or plastic pouches that were the usual receptacles for distribution.

Three of Lam's friends corroborated Ruby's testimony about Lam's bingeing habits, paranoia, and snake fixation, but all three, when cross-examined by Boudreau, were impeached rather comically. Each claimed he had never bought any drugs from Lam, never saw him sell drugs to anyone else, didn't know where he got them, didn't smoke with him, simply went to the apartment to watch TV.

A neighbor recalled seeing Lam scamper out to the street one evening in his underwear, bleeding profusely, screaming. She called the police, who took him to the hospital. Lam told the admitting nurse he'd run through a sliding glass door, trying to get away from the snakes. He was transferred to the county mental health clinic, where he'd been held five previous times for acute cocaine intoxication.

The Chinese officer who had booked Lam on June 23 recounted their conversation in the police station. Lam spoke to him in Cantonese and insisted he had not known it was Simon he was hitting, he'd seen snakes, that he would have never done anything to hurt the kid.

Finally, Hank brought Dr. Jeffrey Winnick to the stand. Winnick, a psychopharmacologist, studied the effects of cocaine on human behavior. He was a frequent consultant to the F.B.I. and the D.E.A., and he had testified in over five hundred trials, mostly—Hank emphasized—for the prosecution. By chance, Winnick had been doing research at Cabrillo State Hospital when Lam was taken there to test his competency. Over the course of four months, he interviewed Lam three times a week for a total of seventy hours.

"Did you arrive at an opinion about Mr. Lam?" Hank asked.

"In my opinion, Mr. Lam was psychotic on June twenty-third and could not appreciate the wrongfulness of his actions. In my opinion, he did not know it was Simon he was beating."

He explained to the jury the psychopathology of freebasing. Because the surface area of the lungs was equivalent to a tennis court, smoking cocaine allowed the drug to enter the bloodstream almost instantaneously, affecting the brain within eight to twelve seconds. The initial effect was as a stimulant, creating a feeling of confidence and euphoria. As one's tolerance increased, however, dysphoria occurred, prompting more frequent usage, which led to paranoia.

"People often begin to have hallucinations at this point," Winnick said, "the most common of which is cocaine bugs. Their brains are firing so fast, these bursts of light—snow lights, they're called—flash in the corners of their eyes, and they think they're seeing things that aren't there, that keep escaping when they turn to look. At the same time, their skin feels like it's prickling, because cocaine constricts the blood vessels, and the combination leads them to believe there are things crawling on them—bugs or worms, or, as in Mr. Lam's case, snakes—and they'll scrape their skin or try to catch them. Since they're wide awake, they'll be absolutely convinced these hallucinations are real, and they'll have delusions beyond the period of intoxication. This stage is referred to as cocaine paranoid psychosis, and it can be latent for months or even years after the last use of cocaine."

"Did Mr. Lam's cocaine habit progress to this stage?"

"Yes. His entire world revolved around trying to prove the existence of these snakes and trying to capture and kill them. He was terrified of them."

"Is cocaine paranoid psychosis caused by an organic disturbance to the brain?"

"Yes."

"So you would say that this is a mental defect?"

"Absolutely."

"Was Mr. Lam suffering from this mental defect on June twenty-third?"

"I am certain that he was."

▪   ▪   ▪

THE jury took two days to reach a verdict, and in the end, they did what was right. Legally, they felt obliged to acquit Lam of child abuse, but they could not absolve him completely of killing Simon. Nor could they find him insane and send him to the relative comfort of a state institution. They convicted him of voluntary manslaughter. Gutierrez sentenced Lam immediately to the maximum term—eleven years.

Hank went to Molly's loft and told her the news. "I should resign," he said.

"Why?"

"I did a great job. On the evidence alone, the jury should've found him not guilty. But they didn't, and I'm relieved. What does that say about me as a public defender?"

"It says you're human. It says Lam got a fair trial."

"With early release, he could be out in six years. He killed a three-year-old kid. Is that fair?"

They went to Banzai Pipeline for sushi, and then stopped by the Moonside Trading Post to rent a couple of videos before returning to the loft. Between movies—two mindless comedies Molly hoped would distract him—Hank popped in the videotape of Molly competing in the N.C.A.A. diving championships fifteen years ago.

"Why are you watching that again?" Molly asked, coming out of the bathroom.

The first time Hank had seen the tape, it had been a revelation, the image of her then. She had saved her best dive for last—a backward one and a half with three and a half twists, ripping the entry, barely bruising the surface. As the crowd erupted, Molly had pulled herself out of the pool. She had knocked the side of her head with the heel of her hand, trying to get the water out of her ear, allowing herself only a small, victorious smile.

"Can you believe I was ever that young?" Molly said. She moved over to the couch, straddled Hank's thighs, and sat on his lap. She locked her arms around his neck. "I have something to tell you," she said. "I decided this a while ago, but I wanted to wait until after the trial. I've decided to have this baby no matter what. With you, without you, regardless of how you feel."

"I suspected as much."

"But I'm hoping you'll be there with me. Do you think you will?"

Hank looked at Molly—her large blue eyes, the freckles across her cheeks, the blond down of eyebrows and lashes. "I don't know," he said. He thought of her standing on the ten-meter platform, not a single tremor or twitch, taut and immortal in her bathing suit. "Our worlds are so different," he said. "You deal with human beings at their highest potential. I see them at their worst."

"What does that mean?"

"How can I say I'll be able to protect this child, when I'm putting people like Lam back on the streets?"

"You can't. But that's the risk we'd have to take. Don't you think it'd be worth the risk?"

They watched the second movie, then fell asleep together. For how long, he did not know. A black, dreamless sleep. Then he awoke to the bed shaking. An earthquake, he thought, as he lay on his back, opening his eyes to the ceiling, scared.

But it was Molly, standing over him at the foot of the bed. "Don't move," she said. He saw her body toppling, breaking the plane of inertia, then falling toward him, gathering speed as she brought her hands together, arms rigid, palms flat. An inch before his face, she split her hands apart, and he felt a rush of air as they brushed past his ears. "You ever do this as a kid?" she asked, holding herself over him. "Admit it. You want this baby."

"What are you doing?"

She stood up and fell again. "Confess."

"I can't be coerced," he said.

"You sure?" She got off the bed. "Don't move."

She walked to the middle of the floor, then turned around. She took two steps, ran toward the trampoline, and bounded into the air. Her back was arched, arms swept out in a swan dive. She was coming right at him. He watched her, staying still. She was going to crush him, he knew. Eventually, she would crush him.

WIDOWERS

A STORM was approaching from the south. Choppy sea, dark sky. Curiously, little wind. It was disquieting, the lack of wind, while the *Reiko II* rode the building swell, dipped and slapped into the whitecaps, the engine—despite the new gasket Alan Fujitani had installed a month ago—humming unevenly.

The woman, Emily Vieira, sat near the stern in the fighting chair, the wooden box with the urn that held the remains of her husband at her feet. Vieira was a Portuguese name, but she was Asian of indeterminate origin, and young, no more than thirty, and very thin. She looked fragile in her coat, which was much too flimsy for February, collar tucked together with one hand, strands of hair escaping from the scarf tied around her head.

Alan had called to her several times: was she sure she didn't want to come inside, stand in the wheelhouse with him where it was warm, where he had a thermos of hot tea steeping? But she had said no, she was all right where she was, and now, as they reached the prescribed three miles and Alan went to her, her face was chapped and reddened from the cold air, eyes staring at the soapy wake of the boat as it dissolved.

"Take your time," Alan said.

She rose from the chair and lifted out the urn. "I'm ready," she told him.

Alan began the service. He said a few words in eulogy, honoring a man and husband he did not know, then opened *The Book of Common Prayer.* "Unto Almighty God we commend the soul of our brother departed, and we commit his body to the deep; in sure and certain hope of the Resurrection into eternal life, through our Lord Jesus Christ—"

Tipping the ashes overboard, Emily whispered, "Back where you belong, you son of a bitch."

"—at whose coming in glorious majesty to judge the world, the sea shall give up her dead; and the corruptible bodies of those who sleep shall be changed, and made like unto his glorious body—"

"Amen," Emily said, abruptly ending the ceremony.

Alan closed the book. "Amen."

Halfway back to shore, she joined him in the wheelhouse. Again, she refused the tea. She stood behind him, leaning against the galley counter. After a few minutes, she pointed to the electronics device to his right and asked, "What's that? Radar?"

"Loran," he told her. "That one's the radar, that's the G.P.S."

She moved forward and removed her scarf. She was even younger than Alan had thought. Twenty-five? Her skin was very pale, unblemished except for a deep inch-long scar above her left eye.

"You want to know something?" she said. "This is the first time I've been on a boat. Well, a tour boat once in San Francisco Bay, but that doesn't count, it was just to Alcatraz. Five years married to a merchant marine, and I've never been on a boat. Can you imagine? I decided to do the, you know, funeral at sea, so maybe I could—" She was at a loss here. "I don't know what I was thinking. He went to a palm reader once. This was years ago. She told Freddy to fear death by water, and he laughed in her face. He always told me he loved it out here."

Alan had read about it in the *Rosarita Bay Horizon*: a three-paragraph article, not in the obituary section, as expected, but presented as one of those human interest stories—brief, piquant, tantalizingly inexplicable. Frederick J. Vieira, thirty-one, fell overboard from the *Shilla Frontier* one night off the coast of Peru. A crew member said Vieira liked to do handstands on the railing. A former state champ in gymnastics, he could hold the position for more than a minute. On the night he went overboard, the water was lulled, glassy. There was the question of suicide. "He just did it for kicks when he got bored," the crew member insisted. "He wasn't depressed or anything." His body was found two days later.

"I guess seamen aren't very superstitious," Alan said to Emily.

She let out a little puff, a scoff. "Yeah."

He was being facetious—seamen were the most superstitious people in the world.

She took a tube of moisturizer from her jacket pocket, squirted some lotion onto her hands, and studiously kneaded her palms and fingers together. "I picked you because you put 'eco-friendly' in the Yellow Pages," she said. "It had a nice ring to it. But you have a diesel engine."

"Yup. Two of them."

"And this boat is fiberglass, not wood?"

"You got me there."

"So what's that mean exactly? 'Eco-friendly'?"

"Wishful thinking?" Alan said. "It's mostly a marketing angle. I do what I can. No discharges, my engines are low-emission, and I use anti-fouling paint and nonphosphate detergents."

"I think I recognize you from the paper. You're on the city council."

"Actually, it's the planning commission."

"You're some sort of environmentalist."

"Not really. Just anti-development." He steered the *Reiko II* toward Rosarita Bay Harbor. "You see Pismo Beach there? I had a beachfront house there that was in my family for four generations—excepting the three years they were interned at Manzanar. The thing is, the house used to be a hundred and fifty feet *inland*. That was before 1959, when the Army Corps of Engineers slapped together the breakwater for the harbor. They never thought about what would happen to the prevailing northwest swell when it hit a concrete wall. Just started pounding away at the beach. Five feet of shore erosion a year. So suddenly they have to reroute Highway 1, and they have to dump tons of riprap on the sand, which does no good, and then my house is on a *bluff,* and then El Niño hits in '92, and it falls into the ocean. People never learn how delicate the ecosystem is."

Emily stared off the port bow at the breakwater.

"Okay," Alan said, "you're sorry you asked."

"No, it's just I've never thought about things like that before. Maybe I'll start recycling now." Playfully, she snapped her scarf at his arm. "How old are you?"

"Forty-seven," he said. "You?"

"Twenty-three," she said, then smirked. "I guess we're both legal."

He didn't know what to make of this comment. Using only his throttles and shifters, he backed the boat stern-to into his slip. Wendell Morishita was jogging down the dock to help with the lines.

"Maybe I'll see you around," she said to Alan, cradling the urn. "I'm starting a job Monday with Gregorio Marine. I'm going to be washing boats. How's that for a twist?" She paid him with cash. "I'm sorry about before, cursing during the service. I haven't seen Freddy in almost two years. He was never around, and when he was, he was a total dick."

Alan watched her walk away. Wendell came aboard and said to him, "Her old man finally bit the dust, huh?"

"You knew him?"

"What are you talking about? Sure I knew him. So did you."

"No, I didn't."

"What's wrong with you? She was always wheeling him around town. You used to say there was some divine justice there, since she ran off with a ball bearing salesman."

"What?"

"Are you drunk or something?"

"A ball bearing salesman?"

"You *know*. He had the stroke right after," Wendell said.

"Who are you talking about?"

They were angry with each other now. "What do you mean?" Wendell said. "*Jack*. Jack Hashimoto. That's his daughter, Laurie Hashimoto."

Alan shook his head. "That wasn't Laurie Hashimoto. Her name's Emily Vieira."

Wendell frowned. "What the fuck. That's not Laurie Hashimoto?"

"No."

"Oh."

They secured the boat for the storm, making fast the bow and stern lines and clearing the bilge.

"Emily Vieira," Wendell said suddenly, nodding his head—it was all coming back to him. "Formerly Emily Ross. Husband killed himself. I didn't put it together—the name change. She went to high school with Suzy. She was fifteen, sixteen, when she got, uh, en*gaged*." He rounded a hand in front of his stomach. "She's Korean, adopted from an orphanage when she was a baby by some fundamentalists. I thought her boyfriend ditched on her."

"Well, you're never wrong when it comes to gossip, are you?"

"Funny," Wendell said. "No, because I heard he bailed, and she got an abortion, and her parents never spoke to her again. He married her?"

"Apparently."

Wendell sucked on his teeth. "I wonder why he did it, why he drowned himself."

The question stayed with Alan, too. Why had Vieira, night after night, balanced himself on the railing, poised upside down, every muscle alert and rigid to maintain the slight arch at the small of his back? Had it been some willful challenge to prophesy, or had he resigned himself to what was deemed inevitable, waiting for the tiniest fluctuation of wind, current, steerage, to tip him over?

▪   ▪   ▪

THEY were both widowers. Wendell had lost Louisa to cancer just three years ago, and Alan, though it had been twenty-two years since Reiko's death, still longed for her with an intensity that, if it were known, would have been thought perverse. They had been almost honeymooners still, married only a year and seven months. She had died of cardiomyopathy, her heart tissue probably damaged by a virus as a kid, undetected until that final morning, when she had collapsed.

Over the years, knowing Wendell and Louisa had pained more than consoled Alan, watching the couple become closer as they raised their children, enduring their pity, especially during holiday meals. Poor Uncle Alan. On occasion, though he knew it was terrible to consider, he was not sorry that Louisa had died, that Wendell's sons and daughter had moved away. There was solace in having Wendell as a fellow mourner, relief in no longer being reminded of what he and Reiko could have had together.

He had made attempts to forget, carry on. Louisa had set him up on dates with her friends, and he met women on his own—thirteen, to be exact, in the last twenty years—but he never thought of remarrying. He sought liaisons that were brief and discreet and held no illusions of love, that were, in simple truth, mere acts of expediency. He ceased to feel guilty about these affairs, nor did he think of them as betrayals to Reiko's memory, yet his life became oddly penitent, as if he believed he deserved his loneliness and misfortune. Even when he and Wendell had been forced out of commercial fishing eight years ago, in effect depriving him of the only vocation he had ever known, Alan had hardly protested.

They had fished for white croaker, sand dab, rockfish, sole, and swordfish, but the big moneymaker had been salmon. Then wholesale prices dropped so low, it wasn't worth leaving port anymore. They simply could not compete with farm-raised fish, the short seasons, the government quotas and regulations. At last count, there had been twenty-four administrators per fisherman. And then, as if they didn't have enough problems, Steller sea lions began popping up in abundance. The cute, mischievous buggers would snatch their salmon right off the hooks—sometimes *eighty* percent of their catch. Before the sea lions were listed as endangered species, fishermen started shooting them with rifles, and Alan had wanted no part in that.

He was among the first to get out of the business, selling his fishing boat and buying a used twenty-seven-foot sport-fisher. He made a modest living with the charters he ran: fishing, weddings, whale watching, burials at sea. The boat was nothing special. The natural teak on the rear deck and exterior trim was a nice touch, but in comparison to his sixty-eight-foot Pacific combo, which had been outfitted for easy conversion, able to long-line, trawl, seine, or troll, depending on the catch and season, it was a toy, a table wine after drinking Château Lafite, dates with divorcées after being married to Reiko.

She had come down from San Francisco to visit an old college friend, and a group of them went to the beach. Louisa was there, too, but Alan and Wendell had paid little attention to her. They steamed clams, played volleyball. Alan stared at Reiko. He liked her neck—long, slender, classical, the smooth nape effulgent when she swept her hair to the side. Wendell, who was vying for Reiko as well, dominated the conversation. She barely looked at Alan.

Later, she wandered away alone for a swim, and Alan followed her, admiring her spirit: the water, even in September, the warmest month, was not much more than fifty-five degrees. She was floating on her back, eyes closed. He waded behind her and cupped her shoulder blades in his hands, holding her afloat while the swells rolled in, lifting her up and down. She had glanced up at him when he first touched her, a queer smile forming, as if she had expected this overture all afternoon, but then she had shut her eyes again, giving herself totally over to his trust, so still he thought she might have fallen asleep. When she stood at last, they kissed. It was the purest moment he would ever know. A month later, he christened his new Pacific combo the *Reiko,* and on the same day, they were married on it.

It was true, what people said: once you experienced perfection, you were ruined.

■   ■   ▥

It rained throughout February and well into March. The weather broke on a Saturday, but the forecast cautioned it would only be a brief respite, another low pressure system moving in that night. Alan made an appointment to have his boat washed, anyway.

Wendell kidded him about it as he rode with Alan to the harbor. "So this is what male menopause looks like," he said.

They parked, and while Wendell repaired to the harbormaster's office, Alan went alone to his boat. On the decks were mops and buckets and the biodegradable cleaning fluids he had requested, but no one was onboard. He scrutinized the work. Many of the rust marks were gone, the chrome shined, the windows were crystalline, and, inside the wheelhouse, everything gleamed. Even the nautical clock and barometer set Reiko had given him for his birthday had been burnished anew. He rubbed his handkerchief over a vestige of polishing solution on the brass.

"Dave warned me to be careful."

He turned to Emily Vieira, who stood outside the doorway, wearing rubber gloves, a white turtleneck, jeans, and an orange slicker stenciled with "Gregorio Marine Maintenance."

"Hm?" he asked.

"My boss told me not to jam through and do a half-ass job, even if it's late and a front's coming."

He joined her on the rear deck. "You're doing fine. Really wonderful work, in fact."

She touched his forearm. "Thanks, Mr. Fujitani."

"How do you like washing boats?"

"It's not bad. Beats cleaning rooms at the Goose Inn. You wouldn't believe the mess people leave behind."

She wasn't exactly pretty, teeth crooked and nose too broad, but today, unlike the first time he had seen her, she was charged with the kinetic energy of youth—bright and blithe. "Are you almost finished?" he asked her.

"I'm done. Well, I've got some more drying to do, but I'm pretty much done. I don't know," she said, glancing over her shoulder, feigning dismay, "you haven't washed this thing in a while, have you?"

"What do you mean? I give it a few passes with a hose every couple of years."

She grinned. "My mistake, skipper."

He helped her carry the cleaning gear down the wharf toward the parking lot. Without reference, she asked, "You married?"

"No," he said.

"You were once, though, right?"

He nodded.

"I could tell. You got that wounded look about you."

They stowed the gear in a bin near the parking lot, and he gave her a check and a large tip. "So," he said, about to say goodbye.

"I'm surprised we haven't bumped into each other," Emily said. "It's such a small town, not a lot of Asians."

"Small towns are like that," he said. "Sometimes you don't see people for months."

"I know. Maybe L.A.'s not going to be a whole lot different in some ways."

"You're moving there?"

"In three weeks."

They stood awkwardly in front of each other, not having any more to say. "I should get going," Alan told her.

"Listen," Emily said, "if you're not doing anything tonight, I've got some halibut. Maybe you want to, you know . . ." She played with the snaps on her jacket, head down. "I don't know, you're probably sick of fish."

"That'd be nice," he told her, flattered.

In the office, Wendell was sitting with Milty, the harbormaster. They were flushed from laughing, finishing a joke. Wendell's chartering business was not doing well lately, but, along with gossip and cussing, he loved a good joke. "Hey," he said to Alan, "sit down, listen to this."

"I'll catch you later, all right?" Alan said.

"What're you talking about? Where you going?"

"Milty can give you a ride."

Wendell came outside. He looked down the wharf at Emily. The reproach was obvious in his face. "Fuck a duck," he said.

"I'll see you later."

"C'mon, Alan, she's a kid."

"I'll see you later."

▪   ▪   ▪

SHE lived in a stucco apartment building, on the second floor. All the apartments faced an inner concrete courtyard, the upper ones accessible by an exterior walkway. Inside her one-bedroom, it smelled musty, like a lakeside house which had collected mildew. She had a green couch, its cushions sunken and frayed, a coffee table, a wicker trunk, an old TV set on a plastic milk crate, fashion and movie magazines scattered on the brown carpet. The one amenity was a working fireplace.

"Can you believe I decorated this myself?" Emily said.

They grilled the halibut on a hibachi outside her front door, basting it with lemon and butter, and mixed a vinaigrette for the fresh tomatoes. Emily made the rice while Alan went to the corner market for beer, French bread, and Duraflame logs.

They ate on the floor, plates on the coffee table, then he did the dishes, giving her a chance to shower. She came out of the bathroom in a long cotton nightshirt, the tails hanging just above the knees. Her hair was still wet, neatly raked with the teeth of a comb. The shirt was all she wore.

"What are you smiling about?" she asked.

"Nothing," he said from the couch.

"Nothing?"

She picked up a bottle of Oil of Olay from the top of the TV and sat on the floor in front of him. She rubbed the lotion on her hands, carefully covering all the skin, including the webs of her fingers and the cuticles.

"You take really good care of your hands," he said.

"My big dream is to be a hand model."

"A what?"

"A *hand* model," she said, waving her fingers. "You know those commercials and ads where you see a pair of hands holding up something, like a jar or a box? Or fingernail polish, diamond rings. Hand models. They make a lot of money doing that."

"And that's what you want to do?"

"I know it sounds stupid. It's like a million to one. But everybody says I've got beautiful hands. What do you think?" She held them in the light of the fire for his inspection.

"They're beautiful," he told her.

"Yeah," she said, staring at them. "The great thing is you can do it forever, even when you get old, as long as you take good care of your hands. I've never been a nail-biter, you know, and I give myself a manicure once a week, a real pro job." She got on her knees and reached for his own hands with the lotion. "Here, let me put some of this on you."

"No, that's okay."

"It's good for you," she said. "I know you think it's kind of faggy, but men should take better care of themselves. See how rough they are? Look, your skin soaks it right up." She stroked her palms over his knuckles.

When they made love, he could smell her shampoo, the Oil of Olay. "How did you know"— she bit into his lip— "when you called Dave, that I'd end up washing your boat?"

"I didn't."

"I guess you just got . . . lucky."

THEY took the *Reiko II* out for a picnic. It was warmer, so they stood on the flybridge, leaning back with the wind as they roared out to sea.

"It must be great to work outdoors, be your own boss," she yelled.

"If you call customers getting drunk and bitching at you all day, if you can call that being your own boss," he said. "They're not referred to as six-pack charters for nothing."

"Look at those clouds. Is another storm coming?"

"No, the wind's turned northwest. That means we're clear of the front."

She hugged him. "I like having a personal weatherman."

"You ever seen the green flash?"

"What's that?"

"It only happens at sunset when the sky's perfectly clear. Just as the sun disappears into the water, there's this little blip of green, like a flashbulb. It doesn't sound like much, but it's incredible. Pretty much only fishermen, people on the water every day, see it, and we'll catch it a dozen times in our lives if we're lucky."

Emily held her hair away from her face. "Freddy had fishing in his blood. His family had a tuna boat in San Diego, but they went out of business when he got out of high school, so he joined the merchant marines."

Alan knew about the tuna fleet in San Diego. They used to set their nets "on porpoise" to fish for yellowfin tuna. They'd locate a pod of dolphins, Pacific spotters or spinners, and they'd lower Zodiacs and pongos—fast, powerful skiffs—into the water to chase them, head the dolphins off and herd them together, like working cattle. Once they encircled the bunch with the fishing net, they'd haul in the purse lines, closing the bottom to trap the yellowfin swimming underneath. The tuna traveled with the dolphins, followed them wherever they went—no one knew why. During each netting, an average of forty dolphins were killed.

Conservationists began picketing the piers with signs: "Would You Kill Flipper for a Tuna Sandwich?," "Murderers." They spray-painted bloody red dolphin silhouettes on sidewalks, posted ten-thousand-dollar rewards for anyone "decommissioning" a boat, released videotapes of porpoises being slaughtered, and called for a nationwide boycott of tuna. Eventually all the major canneries caved in and agreed to buy only "dolphin-safe" tuna, which meant the end for U.S. tuna fishermen.

"Freddy mostly worked on L.N.G. tankers," Emily said, "but he always wanted to go back to fishing. Last year he signed up with a Korean tuna boat. That's what he was doing in Peru. He called me up the week before he fell overboard. He was drunk, babbling something about how he'd killed everything he'd ever touched. We got into a car accident when I was five months pregnant." She pointed to the scar on her forehead. "He was driving. I miscarried and couldn't have any more kids, and he never got over it. He turned mean after that. Beat me once in a while, the jerk."

That she didn't use a stronger epithet made her sound feeble—adolescent—and, at the same time, doubly profane.

▪   ▪   ▪

AT his house, he played a Charlie Parker album on the stereo. Emily came out of the kitchen, carrying a plate of sliced apples and Gouda cheese. "What's that?" she asked.

He told her. "Do you like it?"

"Yeah," she said. "I haven't listened to much jazz, but I like this."

"My wife and I used to go up to San Francisco all the time for concerts. Miles Davis, Sonny Rollins, we tried to see as many as we could."

"When did you guys split up?"

"We didn't. She died. She had a congenital heart defect."

"Oh." She brushed her fingers through his hair. "You never told me that."

"Well," he said, "it was twenty-two years ago."

"You never got married again?"

"No."

"Tell me more about her. What'd you do after the concerts?"

He sipped his wine. "We'd hang out at North Beach, cafés like Vesuvio's, the Trieste, the Savoy. She was sort of a hippie when she was younger so she knew all those places."

"How old was she?"

"She was thirty-one. I was your age—twenty-three."

"An older woman, huh? What is it with men? When you're young, you go for the, you know, the mature, sophisticated type. When you're old, you—"

"I'm *old*?"

"When you're older, you go for bimbettes. Baby-sitters, Catholic schoolgirls. I bet you would've loved me in my plaid skirt and knee socks."

"You went to parochial school?"

"Until I was fifteen. I was adopted by Catholics. Very devout."

"You still go to mass?"

She recoiled, shivered. "Anyway, why should I when I have you? You're sort of like a priest, right?"

He was bewildered.

"You do burials at sea. You marry people, don't you?"

"I'm nothing like a priest."

She began unbuttoning her shirt. "Bless me, Father, for I have sinned—"

"Hey, cut it out," he laughed. "You're making me uncomfortable."

She moved toward him. "Give us this day our daily bread."

　　　　　■　　　　■　　　　■

HE made a call to Earth & Sea, an environmental watchdog group. Freddy Vieira's boat, the *Shilla Frontier*, was a 220-foot purse seiner with a crew of eighteen. It could carry a thousand pounds of frozen tuna—a quarter of a million dollars' worth.

In the last few years, owing to NAFTA, the U.S. had quietly loosened the definition of "dolphin-safe" for foreign fleets. Boats could resume setting on porpoise if they used the backing-down procedure, putting ships in reverse after the seine had been pursed, dragging the far end of the net down to allow the dolphins to swim free. Yet, panicking, the dolphins still got entangled, their snouts and fins stuck in the webbing, or they wouldn't leave their mates, their young, and they'd drown.

Alan began dreaming about them. He dreamt a group of dolphins, netted together, were sinking to the bottom. Frenzied, they twisted over one another, flukes beating. Alan and Freddy Vieira were caught among them. The dolphins gnawed on their limbs, their throats.

▪ ▪ ▪

AT the planning commission meeting, it was the same old story. A developer, Jason Chu, was once again appealing the commission's denial of his project, bringing in a new environmental impact report that was clearly bogus. Alan had been appointed to the commission a year ago, and this was already Chu's third appearance.

"You've got a terminal case of NIMBYism here," Chu said. "Not in *my* backyard. Well, without projects like this, where are the jobs going to come from? What about investment and tax dollars? Your infrastructure? You're letting this town stagnate and die."

They voted five-to-two to uphold the decision.

After the meeting, Alan met Wendell at the Lone Night Cantina, where they usually played dominoes on Monday nights. Alan humored Wendell by coming to this bar. He hated the sappy cowboy music.

Alan planned to take Emily to a Marcus Roberts concert in San Francisco on her final weekend and needed Wendell to handle a charter for him.

"People are beginning to talk, you know," Wendell said.

"What people?"

"You might not care, but you could give the girl some consideration."

"I guess you're right. She probably won't get into the country club now, will she?" Alan said.

Wendell let out a prolonged breath. "How long do you think it'll last? You're going to get tired of her eventually, just like the rest of them. You know that, don't you?"

"If anyone's going to get tired, it'll be her. She's young. You know how it is. Maybe she's out right now with somebody else—her boss, Dave. Maybe she's just sponging me for money. Why else would she be interested in me? Maybe I'll be the one who ends up hurt. Did you ever think of that?"

"You should just break it off now, before it goes too far," Wendell said. "She's been dumped on enough. Think about what she's been through."

Alan could have told Wendell that Emily was leaving in a week, but he did not want to end the argument. "Don't you get lonely, Wendell?"

"Don't be stupid," he said. "Yeah, I do, but do you see me going around—" He drew his lips together. "Admit it. You couldn't give a shit about the girl. You haven't given a damn about anything since Reiko. You've been frozen in this rut. And the fucking thing is, you don't want anything to change. Preservationist, my ass."

⸱⸱⸱　　　⸱⸱⸱　　　⸱⸱⸱

THEY spent Saturday in the city, sightseeing, staying in a hotel on Van Ness, and the next morning drove to a bed and breakfast in Point Reyes. The concert was that night. On Monday, he would see her off at the bus station.

They hiked through the hills until midafternoon, then sat on a blanket on Drakes Beach. It was still chilly, but the storms had passed, the sun out and radiating the white cliffs beside them. They drank from a bottle of wine they'd brought, happy to have the place to themselves. Tipsy, Emily took a short nap, draping her thigh over Alan's legs and nestling against his body. He watched her sleep. Her eyes fluttered underneath her lids, dreaming. When she awoke, she was playful and amorous, kissing him. She stood and removed her jacket. "Let's go swimming," she said.

"You're out of your mind."

"Come on," she said, tugging on his arm. "This'll probably be my last time up here."

"The water's freezing."

"I'm going in!" she called, already sprinting away from him, wearing only her underwear. She dove into a wave and screamed from the cold. "It's wonderful!" she said.

He refilled his wineglass and watched her. He thought again of that day at the beach with Reiko. The memory was becoming strangely artificial to him, pristine in its clarity to the point of being unreal, ridiculously sentimental.

Emily surfed in on a wave, wheeling her arms into the white foam. "That was a big one!" she yelled.

Perhaps it hadn't been that perfect. Perhaps he had accidentally dipped Reiko's head below the surface when she was floating, causing water to get up her nose, and she had darted her eyes at him in sudden doubt, maybe even in fright—the identical look with which she had died, twisting to the floor. He had glanced up from his chair, the newspaper still in his hands, not even able to think yet how odd it was that she was falling.

Emily ran up to him. She shook her hair, spraying water on his face. "Aren't you going to join me?" she asked.

"No way," he laughed.

"You don't know what you're missing." She sprinted back into the ocean, screaming. Such youth. No matter what happened, in Los Angeles or beyond, she would prevail; he was sure of it.

"Alan! Alan!" Emily shouted. "C'mon, come join me!"

He stripped down to his boxers and walked into the frigid sea. He kept his torso turned as the waves crashed into him, then waded to where Emily was splashing gleefully. "Isn't it wonderful?" she asked.

"I've never been colder in my life."

"Here, I'll warm you up," she said. She wrapped her arms and legs around him. She was absolutely exultant, even with her lips bluing. "You see, you get used to it."

He knew he would never have Emily's strength. He would learn nothing. It was too late for him to be lessoned.

"Float on your back," he told Emily.

"What?"

"Your back. Lie on your back for me."

He buoyed Emily under her shoulders as she floated. "This is nice," she said.

Already he could feel his doubts pass. Already, looking down at Emily, he could see Reiko there, and he held her above the swells, his hands steady and relaxed, as if nothing could ever disrupt their tender and elegant suspension.

THE LONE NIGHT CANTINA

THE LONE Night Cantina was not a real cowboy bar. In those places, imagined Annie Yung, in those roadside joints outside of Cheyenne or Amarillo, just off a two-lane highway with pickups made in the good ol' U.S. of A. parked in the dirt lot, the men angled their sweat-stained Stetsons over the eyes and were the picture of stoic reserve. They stood leaning the small of their backs against the counter, an elbow crooked behind for support, pelvis swung out, a boot crossed at the ankle to touch the floor with a dusty, permanently curled toe. Once in a while a cowboy removed the Camel dangling from the corner of his mouth, flicked some ashes, and raised his Bud for a slow swig, condensation from the bottle leaving a wet imprint on his jeans, but otherwise there was no movement, no justification for the odd sense of expectancy and danger in the bar, the feel-

ing that with a single misguided look, anything could happen.

"You're dreaming," Annie's sister, Evelyn, had told her.
"This lonesome cowboy thing, it's all a myth. It's something
straight out of the movies."

At thirty-eight Annie was old enough to know that her
sister was right, and although she also knew that the only
real cowboy who had ever set foot inside the Lone Night
Cantina was its owner, Rob Wilson, and he was too much
the gentleman to wear his hat with the big scoop brim
indoors, the knowledge had not stopped her from coming
here for four nights in a row. Despite its location in
Rosarita Bay, which was as suggestive of the American West
as a piña colada, despite the fact that the bar was usually
dead quiet, lucky to draw the handful of people it had this
Friday night, the place possessed, as she had tried to explain
to Evelyn, the right feel. The bridles and ropes hanging
from the walls, the jukebox stacked with the best of the
country and western standards, the long oak bar counter,
smoothed down in warps where forearms had rested to cra-
dle drinks, the small framed photograph of Rob during his
rodeo days, chasing a calf on his horse, swinging a flat
hornloop over his head—everything gave Annie the impression that, at least for a few hours, she was where she
thought she belonged, in the cheatin' heart world of Loretta
Lynn and Patsy Cline songs, in one of those rotted-wood,
corrugated-tin, hole-in-the-wall, spit 'n' sawdust saloons in
the desert which had a screen door that banged too hard
but no one bothered to fix.

"LOOK at this face," Rob Wilson said, laying the *Daily World News* on the bar counter so Annie could see. He tapped the picture of Delores Hoots when she was fifteen—beaming with honey-eyed innocence for the high school photographer. The adjacent picture was of an old woman, hair shock-white, eyes ablaze and teeth bared in a demented snarl. The headline read: "Father Locks Daughter in Basement for 30 Years for Necking!"

"Believe that?" said Rob. "Maybe in a backwoods town, with a Baptist preacher for a father, but in Chicago? A respected lawyer?"

"I guess you can never tell about people," Annie said.

Rob nodded. "Guess not."

She laughed. "You don't really believe these things, do you?"

"No, of course not. I know it's all made up. I was just, you know, flipping through it. Somebody left it behind."

They both looked at the pictures again. "How'd they find her?" Annie asked finally.

"It says the old man had a heart attack, just keeled over in the office on his desk, and when they went to the house, they saw the door to the basement was locked. She couldn't even talk, had her own, you know, feces smeared on her and scars all over from clawing herself. They said she'd probably been in there since right before her sixteenth birthday. Thirty years in a soundproof room with only a toilet and a cot for company."

"Jesus," Annie said, ratcheting up her howdy-doody

accent. "No wonder she looks like she's got jalapeños for brains."

"It's a shame, huh? Such a pretty girl. All she did was kiss a boy in a car. There's some story that it all had to do with the mother running off with another man."

Annie feigned exasperation. "That's always the story, ain't it? The fault always goes to the woman when the man's to blame."

"You gotcha," Rob said. He squinted at Delores Hoots once more, blew out a silent whistle, and pantomimed a shiver of bloodcurdling proportions, then pointed to Annie's empty glass. "Ready for another?"

"Sure."

She watched him fix her tequila sunrise. His hands—creases on the enlarged knuckles like rough grain on dried wood—were surprisingly graceful, something Annie had noticed when she came to the bar for the first time on Tuesday. Rob had been polite but restrained with her then, called her "ma'am" and questioning only what she wanted to drink. He opened up to her once she indicated she wouldn't mind a bit of chatter—asking if that was him in the framed photograph, if he'd been in the rodeo. "Well, I guess I did a little riding here and there," he had said. Annie told him she was in town to visit her sister, Evelyn, who taught math at Longfellow Elementary School, and he had said, "Hey, my son had her as his teacher, I think. Miss Yung, right?" He gave her a drink on the house, introduced her to his wife when Paquita stopped in later, and on each of the three nights that followed, he treated Annie more and more like a regular, warming up to her without the need to inquire why she was there, alone, a Korean-American database programmer from Silicon Valley who had never been anywhere near a dude ranch, yet who was wearing shiny gray buckskin cowboy boots and a red-sateen, western-cut shirt tucked into tight Levi's, who was talking like a she-hick buckaroo, and who was sporting a bleached-blond hairdo that looked for all the world like a plastic stalagmite.

Annie's sister, however, was not being as tolerant as Rob. Earlier that night Annie had gone into the dining room, where Evelyn was grading tests, and had asked, "How's this look?" She spun a full turn on her toe to show off her outfit.

"You're going there again," Evelyn had said evenly.

"Course I am. Do I look all right?" She went to the hutch, slid a stack of plates aside, and, bending at the knees a bit, examined her face in the mirror between shelves. She yawned her mouth open to trace on lipstick, then pursed her lips on a Kleenex. She drawled in a lollygagging accent vaguely reminiscent of the Southwest, but sometimes slanting toward Dixie Southern and other times dipping into the folk talk of the Appalachian hills, ending her lines with a lilt, as if the tenuous nature of life required that even the simplest statement be posed as a question: "You know what I found out? You see these big ugly gums stickin' out here? Whenever I smile? Look, if I just put the tip of my tongue like this, awn de woof of my mouth when I smile? See? No more pink gubers flashin' like a retard jackrabbit."

Evelyn, her patience running dry, had said, "I thought all of this was—well, cute at first, but don't you think it's gotten a little out of hand?"

Primping her hair, Annie sang, "I can't fathom what you mean, honey."

"Will you stop talking like that for just one second? Please?"

Lowering her hairbrush, Annie had stared at her sister, thinking how little they resembled each other: Evelyn— younger by four years—small, slender, and contained; Annie with her wide face, her plentiful behind, her breasts so full she was often mistaken for fat when her waist had never been larger than twenty-six inches. "If you don't want me here, I'll leave, okay?" she said to Evelyn.

Sighing, her sister slumped back in her chair. "Oh, come on, Annie, you can stay here as long as you want. You know that. It's just that I'm worried about you, that's all. This Dolly Parton thing is really strange."

Annie wet her finger in her mouth and pasted down an eyebrow. "Dolly Parton sucks dogs. Try Kitty Wells, Tammy Wynette even, anyone but that cow," she said.

"Is this—are you doing this because of Bobby?"

Bobby Cho was the systems engineer Annie had been living with for the past three years. She had yet to tell Evelyn that Bobby had proposed to her, and that she had turned him down, after which he accepted a long-standing job offer from a company in Bellevue, Washington. "No, Ev, it's not because of Bobby. I told you, I'm not busted up about it."

"Why'd you break up with him all of a sudden? What did he do? I always thought Bobby was so nice."

"You and everyone else." She was sick of hearing how great Bobby was—gentle, sweet, adoring, solvent, not terrible-looking. "Just let me have my fun, okay?" Annie said.

Evelyn regarded her ruefully and said, "Your hair, it looks awful."

She had bleached it blond a week ago, the evening after she had taken Bobby to San Francisco International for his flight to Seattle. The next day, no longer able to stand their empty apartment in San Jose, she had decided to visit Evelyn, and, driving over the hill on Highway 71, she picked up a country station—transmitting weakly from Salinas—on the car radio. They were broadcasting "Crazy" as part of an all–Patsy Cline special. Annie had heard country music before, but never with this pure, deep-voiced insistence of truth which, at exactly the right moment, would crack and quaver and break your heart. "Walking After Midnight" came on afterward, then "I Fall to Pieces" and "Lonely Street," and, as Annie listened on through the squawk and static, constantly having to wobble the radio dial, she felt as if she had been hit by religion. There it was, she marveled. There it was. Every bane of life imaginable: dreaming, hurting, leaving, and lying, cheating, missing, drinking, loving, and crying. Mawkish and melodramatic, but the pain was real.

When she arrived in Rosarita Bay, she bought every Patsy Cline CD she could find and mooned around Evelyn's house all day, playing song after song, only going out to get more CDs, her devotion growing to include Emmylou Harris, Kitty Wells, and Hank Williams. Then by chance on Tuesday, trying to park near Tommy's Tunes, she turned off Main Street onto Sutter Road and saw the Lone Night Cantina—its name in red neon tubes designed to look like ropes—and just like that, she had a place in which, she could imagine, lived the soul of those plaintive country songs, a place where losers in love could knock back disappointment with a couple of cold ones, where the unlucky and the forsaken could commiserate in holy, countrified silence. She had found, as Patsy Cline had bidden, a place to sit and weep.

 ▪   ▪   ▪

IN the old days there was a superstition among sailors: when you crossed the equator for the first time, you pierced your earlobe and stuck a gold ring in the hole. The tradition was gradually abandoned, but Joe Konki, as he traversed the equator off the north shore of Papua New Guinea two years ago, had had his ear pierced anyway, an Aussie named Shank ministering to him with two ice cubes and a needle sterilized by a Zippo lighter. The inside of the gold earring was engraved later with the longitude, 147° E.

Annie didn't learn any of this for a few hours, but she did notice the earring when Joe first walked into the Lone Night Cantina. She liked it. She liked everything about him, in fact. He was rangy, a lean six-two with straight brown hair parted somewhere near the middle and swept back casually, as if he had run his hand through it for so long, his hair just grew that way now. He had a tanned, narrow face, the evidence of about forty hard-worn years beginning to line the skin, recessed sockets making the eyes seem dry and black, and a square chin you couldn't chisel any better. To Annie, he was perfect. With his leather jacket, black T-shirt, bandy-legged jeans, and scuffed cowboy boots, he was the lonesome stranger personified, a living testament to when men were men.

Flapping the rain off his jacket, he surveyed the bar from

where he stood beside the door, glancing at the only other customers, two young couples at a table. Then Joe looked straight at Annie, who was straddling a stool and looking straight at him, but his gaze passed right over her to Rob Wilson. As Joe strode up to him, Rob, wiping the suds from his hands with a towel, said, "What can I get you?"

"You serve any food here?" His voice was granular and had a trace of a drawl she couldn't quite finger.

"Sorry. All I got for you is Beer Nuts."

"Okay, a bag of those and a Corona." He took off his jacket. There was a tattoo of a dragon, once indigo and now faded to a kind of smalt blue, on his right forearm, and a Rolex watch on his left wrist. No ring.

"Howdy," Annie said sprightly.

He turned to her slowly, as if he wasn't sure she was speaking to him, studied her with curiosity, and said, very flatly, "Hi." He turned back, tugged several crumpled dollar bills out of his jeans pocket to pay Rob, and moved across the room to a table in the corner. Annie watched him prop a boot on a chair, take a swallow of his beer, and open the bag of nuts.

The song on the jukebox, "Pancho and Lefty," ended, and Annie lifted two quarters from her pile of change on the counter and crossed the room to the machine. She took her time picking a song. Finally she dropped one of the quarters into the slot and punched the buttons for Kris Kristofferson's "Help Me Make It Through the Night." She waited for the record to begin, flipping the second quarter in the air, then, with the coin held loosely in her palm, she lazily twirled around as if to go back to her stool. The quarter flew out of her hand and pinged, bounced, and slid until it came to a stop not more than three feet from Joe's table in the corner, exactly where she had planned.

Sheepishly Annie walked over and retrieved the quarter and, as she was straightening up, said to him, "I've got butter for hands." He regarded her blankly. He popped a nut into his mouth and crunched down on it. She touched the back of the chair occupied by his boot and asked, "Mind if I sit down?"

"Huh?"

"Use some company?" she asked in her best cowgirl lilt.

He stared at her expressionlessly. Perhaps five full seconds passed before he lifted his foot and let her take the seat.

She extended her hand. "My name's Annie Yung."

He gave her a limp shake. "Joe."

"Joe what?"

"Konki."

"Pleased to meet you, Joe Konki." In her nervousness, she forgot the trick of using her tongue and flashed a big, toothy, salmon-pink gum smile. "Where you from? You ain't from around here, are you?"

He shook a Newport from his pack and lit the cigarette with a match. He blew out smoke, and said, "Florida, originally."

"Yeah? What parts?"

"Gainesville."

"So you're just passing through Rosarita Bay or something?"

He nodded. "Had some business to take care of here. Heading to San Diego in the morning."

"San Diego. That where you living now? Or you going back to Gainesville?"

"I don't know. I just got back to the States a couple of nights ago. I was overseas, in Indonesia, for the last two years."

"Yeah? Doing what?"

He drank from his Corona. "I worked boats in the Molucca Islands."

Annie fancied the idea: it was exotic and adventuresome; he had found the frontier exhausted but had kept going west. "Must've been humid as hell down there," she said to him.

He tilted his head back. "Why are you talking like that?"

"Like what?"

"Like some yahoo." He leaned across the table and brandished his watch. "That accent's about as real as this Rolex."

"Listen, let's just forget it," Annie said, standing up.

"Hey, sit down, sit down," he said. He ran his hand through his hair. "I wouldn't mind talking to you, but let's be straight with each other, all right?"

She remained standing. She didn't know what she had expected from him, but she certainly had not thought he would confront her like this.

He was smiling at her now.

Grudgingly, she said in her normal voice, "All right."

"Let's start over," he said. "My name's Joe Konki."

She settled back down in the chair. "My name's Annie Yung."

▪   ▪   ▪

THEY sat in the Lone Night Cantina and talked for close to three hours. He told her about his short-lived boxing career out of high school, traveling the club circuit in Florida until he fought a southpaw and didn't keep his right up to protect his chin. After the jawbone healed, he enlisted in the Navy, making ports of call in the Philippines, where he had the dragon tattoo drawn on his arm, in Japan, and even in Korea.

"Hangul mal chokum aro?" Annie asked. Do you know a little Korean?

"Uh, *kamsa-hamnida,*" Joe said. Thank you.

After his tour was up, he returned to Gainesville, where he worked construction for ten years. Then he moved to Louisiana, Morgan City, and got a job offshore on the rigs. He enjoyed the life, seven days on and seven days off, the hurricanes and Cajun food and whipping chains, but he had this hankering to go somewhere, and on a whim he took off to Southeast Asia, tramp-steaming between Menado, Amboina, and Banjermasin.

"One time," he said, "we heard on the radio that a cargo ship lost three containers in the water, and we raced over there, thinking V.C.R.s, oh, man, fur coats, and what do we find when we open them up? Cocoa Puffs. Three containers—forty-footers each—of Cocoa Puffs."

"It almost sounds like you were a pirate on the high seas."

"No, mostly it was smuggling," Joe said.

Annie raised her eyebrows.

"Joking," he said.

"Sure you are," she said. "You know, Rosarita Bay has an outlaw history. My sister told me during Prohibition the town was filthy with rumrunners and bordellos."

"You'd never know it, looking at it now."

"You got that right."

He said he didn't have a clue where he'd go from here. He

had recently come into an unexpected windfall—he alluded to some sort of an inheritance—and would use the money to travel. He'd go to San Diego to visit some old naval buddies, then Vegas, then Houston to see his mother, then maybe Europe.

Annie told him that in comparison to his life, hers had been fairly dull. Strikingly normal, actually. Grew up across the Bay in Walnut Creek, went to Caltech, and had worked for a series of software companies in the Silicon Valley. Now, like everyone else, she was on the Internet bandwagon. "It's not as glamorous as you might think," she said. "I'm going blind, looking at all those lines of code."

She had been married twice in her twenties. Her first husband had left her for another woman, her second had left her for another man.

"You're kidding," Joe said.

"Sadly, no."

The first marriage—right after she graduated from Caltech—had lasted all of a year. Phillip Han had been her roommate's brother, and he was like no Korean she had ever met. He taught hapkido, wore a ponytail, rode a Harley, and wanted to be a movie star, the next Bruce Lee. He was wild, fun, and very, very cool. He was also terrible with money, squandering all of hers since he didn't make any, and he was an inveterate philanderer. Annie came home one night to find him in bed with two coked-out starlets, and Phillip was unrepentant, telling her, "Man, you are such a drag. Get the fuck out of here, you fat cow."

Her second husband, Nils Sigridsson, was a middle-aged Swedish architect with a gorgeous house in Sunnyvale. He had impeccable taste and manners, and they spent summers antiquing up and down the coast and winters skiing in Tahoe, where he patiently tutored her on the bunny slopes. All was perfect, until he became impotent. They began trying things, benign attempts at being risqué escalating to porn videos and rape fantasies, anal sex and bondage. They entered couples therapy, and Nils fell in love with another husband in the group, a lapsed Mormon podiatrist.

Annie told none of this to Joe—it wasn't her favorite subject—instead asking, "You been married?"

"Once."

"What happened?"

"Let's just say it ended badly, too."

They got on the topic of bad dates, and Annie had plenty to recount—a lot of them with white men afflicted with A.H.F., Asian Hottie Fetish, wanting her to titter with high-cheeked China-doll timidity, or vamp it up as a wanton Suzie Wong, a dirty little yum-yum girl. "You've spent a lot of time in Asia," she said to Joe. "You're not like that, are you?"

"No," he said, blushing.

Then there was the guy she met at a party who asked her out, and who, on their date, said, "You know, I usually only go out with beautiful women, but you're so *funny.*"

And she couldn't forget Juan Pablo Sevilla from Chile. He had whispered endearments to her in bed, *querida mía, niña bonita, linda,* his baritone a fluttering seduction, corny but nonetheless effective, making her squirm whenever she heard it. His gift, his great secret as a man and a lover, he told people, was this: the simple knowledge that to want to please a woman was enough; it showed he cared, whether he did or not. Annie was beginning to fall for his machismo, but his friends, whenever she was introduced to them, kept asking her if she'd met Juan Pablo's sister, Gabriela. It was very mysterious. Even more so when Gabriela visited from Santiago, and she was all over Juan Pablo. It was unnatural, their affection for each other. Annie finally asked Juan Pablo, "Is there something going on between you and your sister?" and he admitted that there was: they were lovers. Had been for many, many years. "It is sex, but not sex," he said. "It is brother-sister. It is—how you say?—chaste, yes?" "No," she said. "Not chaste."

"I'm glad you can laugh about all this," Joe told her.

"Believe me, I cry about it, too."

"Was your last boyfriend some sort of cowboy?" Joe asked. "I've been meaning to ask you about the honky-tonk outfit."

"No, he wasn't," Annie giggled, thinking of roly-poly Bobby Cho as a cowboy. "I'm just having your everyday nervous breakdown."

"I can respect that."

She glanced up at Joe, liking him enormously for saying that.

"Looks like we're closing the place down," he said. The two young couples across the room were putting on their coats to leave.

"Maybe we should go soon," Annie told him. "Let Rob go home."

He nodded.

"Where you staying? Need a ride?" she asked.

"I'm around the corner at the Goose Inn."

Annie chewed on a cuticle, then asked shyly, "You want to continue this conversation? Maybe in your room?"

"You sure?"

"Just give me a minute," she said.

She went to the back of the bar and used her cell phone to call her sister.

"Hello?" Evelyn answered.

"I got lucky tonight, sis."

"Annie? Where are you?"

"I hooked me a sailor," she said. "I ain't gonna be home tonight, honey."

"Are you going to be okay?" Evelyn asked. "Do you know what you're doing?"

"I'm a big girl," Annie said, not hiding her annoyance. "You know, we used to be so close. When'd it get like this?"

"Don't drive if you've been drinking," Evelyn told her, and hung up.

■   ■   ■

IN the Goose Inn, he lay on top of her, face buried in her hair. "I can't do this," he said.

"Tell me what to do," Annie said.

"No, it's not that." He rolled away and swung his legs off the bed. "Listen, you mind if we get dressed?"

Annie went to the bathroom to put on her clothes. As she fastened the hooks and eyelets on her bra, she peered at herself in the mirror. She looked a mess. Black roots were showing at the part on her hair, her makeup was smudged, there were bags under her eyes. She planned to say goodbye and leave quickly, saving them both further embarrassment, but when she came out of the bathroom, she hesitated, seeing Joe in the chair beside the desk, holding a folded piece of paper between his fingers, sunk into himself, lost. She took a seat on the edge of the bed.

"There's a bridge outside of town, in the marsh, where Highway 1 crosses a canal," he said. He handed her the folded piece of paper. "Take a look at this."

It was an Allstate Insurance check, made out to Joe in the amount of $50,000. She gave it back to him.

"This is the reason I was in town today," he told her. "To pick this up. Last winter, Kathy was driving on that bridge. There was an accident, somebody trying to pass a truck, coming right at her. She swerved, went off the bridge, drowned trapped in the car. I didn't even know she'd been living here. I didn't know where the hell she was, and I didn't care. I hadn't seen her since we were twenty-seven. I don't know, it came out of the blue. I never understood it. One day she just took off. I didn't know what'd happened to her. I was worried sick, I thought maybe she'd been in a wreck or kidnapped by some maniac. Put out a missing person's report, but the police said she wasn't in any of the hospitals or the morgue. I was going out of my mind. Then, a week later, I came home from work, and there she was, drunker than piss on the couch, and over there at the dining table was her boyfriend, scared shitless, looking at me and swearing he didn't know she was married. I yanked the son of a bitch up, ready to whale on him, and he could barely stand, he was so fucking wasted. I could tell from his breath he'd just puked, and he said to me, 'Listen, it wasn't my doing, understand? If you're going to beat the shit out of someone, beat the shit out of her.'

"Later, I found out about it, I found out the facts. She'd gone to Fort Lauderdale and picked the guy up. He was a welder or something, just some guy in a bar. They shacked up in the Ramada Inn for the entire week. Never left the room. Just stayed in there and fucked and drank tequila like it was a honeymoon. They got kicked out of the hotel, and she told him to come back with her to Gainesville. It was deliberate. She'd planned it. She wanted me to see what she'd done, so she brought the son of a bitch to our house. I didn't know any of that. I didn't find all that out until later, but right then, I knew the guy was telling the truth. I knew he was right about Kathy, about who was to blame, and I should've let him go and said to hell with it, but I looked down at her passed out on the couch, her tit hanging out of her dress, and I went crazy. I broke the guy's face in, busted two ribs. I nearly killed him.

"I got put in jail for six months, and around the second month, Kathy came to visit me. I wouldn't see her, told the guard to tell her to go to hell. She didn't come back. When I got out, I heard she'd left town. Never saw or heard from her again. Then here it is, almost fifteen years later, and I'm in Indonesia, and I get this telegram saying she'd been in an accident. It took them over a year to track me down."

For a moment, he was speechless, shaking his head. "She'd made me her beneficiary. Fifteen years I hadn't seen her, and she made me her beneficiary. I don't get it." He stared at the Allstate check. "What am I supposed to think now? Did she still love me? The only way I could get through the last fifteen years was to blame her, to think she hated me for God knows what reason. Why else would she've brought that guy to the house? I think to myself, maybe she left me the money so I'll always wonder, maybe it's part of her hate. But I don't know anymore. Maybe I was wrong. Maybe she still loved me."

They sat silently in the room. There was nothing Annie could tell him.

Joe said, "I just wanted you to know, it had nothing to do with you. You're a pretty woman."

▪   ▪   ▪

IT was raining hard, the wiper blades squeaking muddy arcs across the windshield. Offshore, sheet lightning flared, illuminating the sky for a suspended second, then leaving Annie in the dark of her car.

She flicked on the radio. Linda Ronstadt singing "Long, Long Time." She turned it off. After waiting for a Chevron truck to clear the intersection, its wheels shaving through the water on the road, she swung into the parking lot of an all-night drugstore on the corner. She ran from her car into the store, where a woman in her sixties with coarse white hair stood behind the counter, reading a magazine. Annie was momentarily spooked, thinking the clerk resembled the woman in the tabloid photo, the one hidden in the basement, Delores Hoots.

"Nasty out, huh?" the clerk asked.

Annie realized she had been wrong, there was no likeness at all. The magnifying effect of the lady's thick eyeglasses had made her appear, in that moment, frightened and lunatic.

Annie walked down the aisles to the hair coloring section. She carefully studied the samples, then picked out a box of Number 36 Midnight, Neutral Black—the closest to her original color she could find.

The clerk, as she was ringing up the purchase, gave out an enormous yawn. "Sorry," she said.

"Long night?" Annie asked.

"Sometimes it feels like a long life," the woman said.

Annie got back in her car and pulled onto Highway 1. She leaned over to the dashboard and raised the heat. Light flickered in the distance. More lightning, she thought, flaring down somewhere far behind her. When she glanced in the rearview mirror, though, she saw a pair of headlights—flashing from low to high beam—rapidly gaining on her, blinding her. Before she knew it, the truck had loomed abreast, the coupling between its two trailers bouncing and rattling, and then it hurtled past her, slapping water on her windshield and barreling down the highway in a contrail of spray and taillights.

She stopped her car on the shoulder of the road, dug her cell phone out of her purse, and called Evelyn.

"Please don't tell me you've been in an accident," her sister said.

"No. I'm just calling so you won't worry. I'm taking a little drive."

"In this weather?"

Annie stared through the windshield at the rain. "Ev?" she said.

"What?"

She wanted to tell her sister what she was feeling—that she

hadn't been living, she had been hiding, that she'd only been with Bobby because she had been afraid of getting hurt, and he had been safe, he would have never cheated on her, or lied to her, or left her, yet she hadn't loved him—but it was so hard for Annie to talk to Evelyn, who at thirty-four had never been married, who, as far as Annie knew, hadn't had a boyfriend in years.

"I'll be home soon," she told Evelyn. "I want to drive some more."

She rooted through the glove box and found a CD by Emmylou Harris, *Bluebird*. She cued the song "A River for Him," then resumed down the road, following the yellow lane reflectors embedded in the blacktop. Lightning lit the sky, and she saw the greenness of the artichoke fields on the side of the highway, the plants large, saturated, ready for harvest. Emmylou's soprano began to float over Annie in a slow, mournful waltz. Rain was thudding against the roof of the car, the wind was making the trees swing and whip.

For the first time in a week, she thought about work. She supposed she had to go back to work. She had missed an important meeting, and she was behind on a beta test. She had to buy some furniture, a new bed. The queen with the bird's-eye maple frame had been Bobby's, and he had taken it with him to Seattle. Annie wished she could keep driving instead. It'd be so much easier to keep driving. She had money; she was vested. She could drive forever.

CASUAL WATER

THERE WAS an airstrip a few miles down the coastal marsh, abandoned and accessible only by boat now, the road bridge washed out by years of storms and erosion and neglect. Impractical as it was, Patrick Fenny's father, Davis, a former P.G.A. golfer, was fond of using the airstrip as a driving range, and Patrick and his little brother sometimes accompanied him during the last two summers, when it had been unusually warm. They would stand on the rippling concrete, three hundred yards of cracked, potholed runway downwind from Davis, and shag golf balls for him with baseball mitts.

Patrick, who was in high school, was the designated fielder, and Brian, seven years his junior, served as backup. They'd watch the balls sing through the thick, paludal air as if fired out of a cannon, like tracer bullets, just dots in the haze and fog, speeding toward them without trajectory. Of course,

Patrick rarely caught any on the fly. The balls came too fast, bouncing down before he could get a bead on them, or they would tail just out of his reach. On the occasions when one was hit directly at him, he'd twist away on instinct, his glove held awkwardly in his stead. As much as he hated his father's reproofs ("Aw, you wuss"—said half-chuckled, half-disappointedly), it would have been disaster if he misjudged the ball, or equally painful if he caught the thing in the pocket of his mitt, which would leave his palm stinging for a week.

But last August, the last time they would go to the airstrip together, Patrick had a day which seemed to make up for all the misses, the endless puffing after balls that bounded past them, the hours of sweaty heat, the gnats and mosquitoes they forever had to wave aside with their gloves. He could do no wrong, flagging down everything that came near him. It was exhilarating, this sudden and perfect ability, and when Davis cracked his longest shot of the afternoon off the tee, a beautiful drive, straight and ascendant, Patrick would swear that he was locked on it from the beginning of its flight, that he could see the dimples of the ball, the brand Titleist, frozen in a slow whirl. He ran back, striding fast, covering impossible ground, and with a smooth swing of the arms and knee, leapt into the air, fully extended, almost horizontal. The ball smacked into the webbing of the glove, and Patrick, dropping to the concrete, was already remembering the sound of it, so sweet and true. He jogged back to Brian, laughing to himself—laughing because he knew it had been magnificent, that catch, and it had been so *easy*. For six and a half seconds, everything—the coordination of mind and body, time and place, the entire cosmos—had fallen into sync. He was nearly euphoric, and he knew that Brian, gawking at him, could intuit something intangibly special about the catch as well.

But they withheld their exultation, they waited, they looked to their father to see what he'd say. Davis, a wavering mirage at the end of the airstrip, faced them mutely. Then, slowly, he let his club drop out of his hand and took a step forward. He thrust both fists into the air and began howling. The boys started howling, too, and pretty soon father and sons were dancing and waving in celebration. At that moment, the two boys, motherless for so long, adored him with a purity akin to pain—this man whose approval they coveted, this man whose love they sought.

THE following spring, in March, Davis abandoned them, and for nearly three months, Patrick kept the fact of his desertion secret, the knowledge weighing down on him, making him inwardly bitter and bereft and terrified. He told everyone that Davis had gone on the Nike Tour—a series of golf tournaments that made up a Triple-A minor league for the P.G.A.—which was partially true, and that he would return sometime soon, which wasn't exactly true, although it was what Patrick wanted to believe.

Patrick was graduating from high school—as the valedictorian, no less—and he was scheduled for induction into the Naval Academy in Annapolis, Maryland, on July 1. Here it was, the first week of June already, and he still didn't know what to do about his eleven-year-old brother, Brian, the pain-in-the-ass little shit whom he loved and had pretty much raised single-handedly, ever since their mother had repatriated to the Philippines eight years ago. Patrick was frozen with indecision. He couldn't take Brian with him to Annapolis—midshipmen weren't allowed to have dependents—and, in any case, still several months shy of his eighteenth birthday, he was ineligible to be Brian's legal guardian. And there were no relatives on Davis's side to speak of, no one still alive with whom they had kept in touch. If Patrick did anything, sought any kind of help or made the most innocent of inquires, he was sure that Brian would be put in foster care, a prospect Patrick dreaded, but knew was inevitable, and chose to deny, praying that his father would have a change of heart and return home before he went to Annapolis.

As it was, Brian decided things for him. On the last day of the school year, in his sixth-grade math class, he inexplicably slammed his head against his desk, splitting his forehead open. His teacher, Evelyn Yung, saw it happen. Throughout the class, she had noticed how quiet and subdued Brain was, and she had wondered why he seemed so sad, when the rest of the kids were giddy anticipating the onset of summer vacation. Then, as the final bell rang, as the other children sprang up, elated, Brian stayed in his chair, staring blankly at the wooden desktop, and, as Evelyn watched, he inhaled and stiffened upright—although she would remember perceiving the motion oppositely, as if he were coiling into a ball—and he flung his head, his entire torso, down. A sick thump sounded across the room, not loudly, but chilling somehow, causing his classmates to stop their delirious exodus and turn to Brian as he rose back up, exhibiting not a hint of pain or shock or mania, absolutely expressionless, as a gash on his skin bloomed apart and blood ran down his face.

Patrick was across town at Clothilde's Bistro, the new French restaurant in Rosarita Bay, prepping for the Friday dinner rush. It was a marked step up, this job as assistant chef, after years as a short-order fry cook at Rae's Diner, and he was lost in the rhythm of his work, marveling as he minced a shallot what a difference a good knife made, the precision-honed German blade slicing through the bulb and tapping against the cutting board as if nothing were there, when Sergeant Gene Becklund from the sheriff's office appeared next to him, looking stupidly lugubrious so at first Patrick assumed the worst. Patrick didn't like Becklund. He was humorless and by-the-book. Two summers ago, he'd arrested Patrick's father for drunk driving, but Davis had been acquitted at trial, which hadn't squared well with Becklund.

On the way to the clinic, Becklund asked questions: Where was their father? How long had he been gone? When was he expected back? How could he be reached? Patrick said he didn't really know. Davis was somewhere in the Midwest or South, and although he'd been checking in every few weeks, he hadn't called him since May.

"He just left you guys to fend for yourselves?" Becklund said.

"He left me some money," Patrick said. "It's not like I've never had to hold down the fort before." Becklund knew this. Everyone did. Davis had a reputation for taking off abruptly for days at a time, even weeks, and these little "business trips" were getting more frequent of late—trips he first claimed were part of a consulting job to help design a new golf course near Palm Springs, but were actually treks to small tournaments, Davis going farther and farther afield to see if he could revive his competitive golf career.

At the clinic, Evelyn Yung was standing outside the room where a doctor was stitching Brian's forehead, and when she saw Patrick, she startled him by hugging him. Without meaning to, he sank into the smell and feel of her, her shampoo, her perfume, her moisturizer, her tiny waist and small, pointy breasts. She had been his elementary school math teacher as well, what seemed like many years ago, and he had had a profound crush on Miss Yung, but he had not spoken to her for quite a while, although he had heard rumors about her, about her and the man who stood behind him, Gene Becklund, married father of three, about their affair and Sally Becklund finding out and kicking him out of the house. When was that? Patrick tried to remember. What had happened? Were they still lovers? As he separated from Miss Yung's embrace, he watched her look at Becklund, watched Becklund look at her, but they betrayed nothing.

"He's going to be okay," she said. "The cut on his forehead, the doctor says it won't leave much of a scar, but he wouldn't talk to me, to anyone, he won't say anything at all."

"Can he leave after they finish?"

"I think so," she said. "Has something been going on at home? Has something been bothering him?"

"My dad's been away. I've been working a lot. Maybe he's been lonely."

"Lonely? It has to be more than that. He intentionally *hurt* himself. You didn't see it. It was horrifying."

The doctor came out into the hallway, and after a brief medical update, Patrick went into the treatment room alone.

Brian was sitting on the gurney table, a large bandage on his forehead, blood caked on his T-shirt and jeans. He stared at his tennis shoes as he dangled and kicked his feet.

"Hey," Patrick said.

"Hey," Brian mumbled back, not lifting his head.

Patrick sat next to him. Together like this, there was no mistaking they were brothers. Although Patrick was thin, while Brian still had some prepubescent pudginess about him, they had the same chestnut-colored straight hair, sallow skin, sprinkle of freckles, and large, sloe eyes. They were good-looking boys, but there was an unsettling otherness about them, their blood mix unusual and somewhat antithetical: Irish, Scottish, Filipino, Malay, with, if Davis could be believed, a little bit of Ojibwa Indian thrown in.

Patrick palmed the top of Brian's head and tilted it back to examine the bandage. "Well, you pain-in-the-ass little shit," he said, "now look what you've done."

▪   ▪   ▪

THE next afternoon, Becklund brought a woman, Julie Fulcher, from the San Vicente County Department of Family and Children's Services, to the house. She was young and athletic-looking, which surprised Patrick, but the fact that she was there did not. Becklund again—by the book.

"You're really out in the middle of nowhere, aren't you?" she said.

They lived in a small three-bedroom rambler off Highway 1, on an access road that didn't have a name. The property was in the middle of the coastal marsh alongside a canal, and there was nothing within miles other than the abandoned airstrip. When Davis had bought the house, he had thought it a great investment; there had been plans for a big new development in the marshland. But Rosarita Bay's planning commission, pressured by environmental groups, had postponed the groundbreaking indefinitely. It turned out that one-fifth of all North American bird species could be found in the marsh, some of them endangered. "Goddamn snowy plovers," Davis would lament.

Julie Fulcher interviewed the boys together briefly, then took Brian aside to talk to him alone, leaving Patrick in the living room with Becklund.

"You could have given me some warning," Patrick said to him. "The place is a mess."

"Sorry. They like to operate that way," Becklund said. "Listen to me, Patrick. The Nike Tour's in Ohio this week, but your father's not there. He hasn't played in a single Nike tournament since January."

"He's not just playing Nike. He's doing other mini-tours. It all depends where he can get exemptions and enter."

"He didn't give you any details when he called last month?"

"We didn't talk long. He was in a rush."

"You know where he kept his records? Bank statements, credit card bills, things like that?"

"I think so," Patrick said, knowing precisely where they were. Over the last year, with his father increasingly negligent, Patrick had taken it upon himself to handle many of the bills—the utilities and the telephone and the everyday expenses—but Davis had withheld the larger financial matters from him. When he left in March, Patrick discovered—

just as he'd suspected—that Davis had been in deep money trouble. He had a load of debt on a dozen credit cards, he'd let the family's Blue Cross coverage lapse, and he was way behind on his mortgage payments. The $5,000 he'd put in an envelope for Patrick—fifty crisp, new one-hundred-dollar bills—didn't make a dent in what they owed. The bank was preparing to foreclose on their property.

Fulcher came out of Brian's bedroom and asked Patrick to take a walk with her. Outside, she said, "Do you even get mail delivered here?"

"We have a P.O. box in town," he told her.

"It must be hard for Brian, being so isolated."

"He sees his friends," Patrick said. "He does sleepovers."

"But after school gets out, you and your father are usually working, right? He's alone all afternoon?"

"I spend time with him. I pick him up from school, and I make sure he's set up with a snack and his homework, and I make dinner for him and my dad to microwave before I leave."

They rounded the corner into the backyard. "Good God," Fulcher said, "what's that?"

It was a 1966 Piper Cherokee, a rusting heap of a seaplane without an engine or propeller, tied up to a tiny dock on the canal behind the house. Davis had bought it on a whim after many years of being harangued by Patrick about flying lessons. They never got around to refurbishing the plane beyond putting in two bucket seats from an old VW bug.

"You want to be a pilot at the Naval Academy, don't you?"

"You don't get into flight training until after you graduate, and even then it's a long shot, but yeah, that's what I want to do."

Fulcher stepped onto the dock and peered at the thirteen-foot Boston Whaler next to the seaplane. "You guys fish?"

"Sometimes."

"Did your father drink a lot?"

Patrick had expected the question. "You've been talking to Becklund."

"How much did he drink a day?"

"A couple of beers. He's not a drunk."

"Did he ever hit you or Brian? Ever threaten you?"

"No."

"He used a lot of rough language around you guys, didn't he?"

"What do you mean?"

"Is your nickname for Brian 'little shit'?"

Patrick stared at her. "You would be a lot better at your job," he said, "if you had a brain in your head."

░   ░   ░

AFTER they finished dinner, Patrick moved to the sofa while his brother cleared away the plates. Brian scraped chicken bones into the cat's food bowl, opened the back door, and called into the dark, "Hey, Lucy. Come on, Lucy."

The cat scurried inside and began chomping on the bones.

"She might choke on those things, you know," Patrick said, glancing through the kitchen doorway.

"No, she won't," Brian said. He squatted down to pet the cat. "She's just going to take the meat off." He straightened up and ran the water in the sink. "Did you get some more detergent?"

Patrick flossed his teeth.

"Well, did you?"

"I forgot."

"You forgot? How am I going to wash the dishes, then?"

"Just leave them," Patrick told Brian. He heard him continuing to clatter plates in the sink. "Hey, I said leave them."

"Okay, okay," Brian said, shutting off the water. "I was just going to rinse."

It had become like this between them, their relationship one of accumulated resentments, bickering over the picayune—unfinished chores, noisy habits. An old married couple, Davis called them.

Brian picked up the cat and sat on the sofa. Absently, he spluttered a few bars of a song through smooched lips. He played trumpet in the elementary school band. He stopped suddenly and asked, "Are we Amerasian?"

Patrick looked at his brother. "Who told you that?"

"The woman. She asked if kids ever tease me because I'm Amerasian."

"We're not Amerasian," Patrick said. "That's what they call people whose mothers are Vietnamese."

"Was Mom a bargirl before she met Dad?"

"What are you talking about?"

"Billy Kim saw it in a movie. That's what they call hookers in the Philippines."

"She wasn't a hooker. She was in college and she worked as a secretary on the naval base. Billy Kim's full of shit." Patrick calmed himself, then said, "What else did the woman ask you?"

"She asked me if I know the difference between good touching and bad touching."

"Jesus," Patrick said. "She's a complete fucking idiot."

"Do you think Dad's going to come back before you leave for the Academy?"

"Sure he will. That's always been the plan," Patrick said, trying, as well, to convince himself. "He just wants to get in as many tournaments as possible—you know, while he still can. It's like his last hurrah."

"He didn't even say goodbye to me," Brian said. "He hasn't called when I've been around."

"I told you. You know how it is when he's on the road."

"If he doesn't come back," Brian said, "are they going to put me in a foster home?"

"No, that's ridiculous. He'll come back, and everything will be fine. Don't let that woman scare you." He waited for his brother to say more, but Brian sat still, stroking the cat. His hair was snagged on the corners of his bandage. "You need a haircut," Patrick told him.

▪   ▪   ▪

DAVIS Fenny had not looked like a golfer. He was too fit, too stocked with muscle, ever to convince anyone that he could delicately chip out of the rough onto a short green, that he could do anything, for that matter, which required patience and restraint. He carried himself with the stand-up, bow-legged, bow-armed gait of a high school fullback or a Marine, both of which he'd been, and though he seemed amiable enough most of the time, one could never dismiss the sense that without provocation, he might fly off the handle: knock over a table while remembering some vague failure, or coldcock someone in a bar. Not the temperament needed for the doglegs, to lay up on an approach shot, say, instead of trying an impossible drive over a water hazard. All in all, he was perfect to hustle golf.

And that was what he did on occasion—not for the cash, simply for kicks. At first, he went to the municipal courses in Santa Cruz or Monterey wearing cutoffs and running shoes, carrying a pitiful Sunday half-bag. He'd walk up to a group and ask bashfully if he could make up the foursome, and hit duck hooks and shank two-irons and putt as if he had a croquet mallet between his hands until he was able to raise the stakes.

Very quickly, though, he switched tactics to what was more natural to his mien, assuming the role of the cocky punk who hadn't grown up, beaming teeth and confidence, always a tip of the baseball cap and a wink for the ladies. "Swoo-eet," he'd breathe after a pretty, young one passed by. He'd go into elaborate, lengthy motions to tee off, sprinkling grass to test the wind, sniffing the air, and rocking on his feet until they were positioned just so. Next he'd squint down the fairway, set his club, sniff, rock, and squint a few more times, and finally go into his backswing, eyes on the ball, hips twisting, legs shifting, ready to really rip one, and . . . he'd stop, just stop, and step away. "I don't know, maybe you fellas want to cover your ears," he'd say, "'cause when I hit this thing, it's going to snap 'em back, it's going to pop your drums like a howitzer blast." He had a rowdy charm, something the suburban duffers couldn't resist trying to squash. He'd tell his sons about each game's unfolding with absolute glee, how he had suckered those butterballs and come through in the clutch with a dream of a shot.

Still, it was a sad outcome for a golfer who had had such promise. As a teenager in Tempe, Arizona, he had been known for the tremendous torque generated by his swing, which would almost yank his shirttails out of his pants. Even in high school, he was all intensity and concentration, and people said he was another Jack Nicklaus, destined for greatness. He was given a full golf scholarship to the University of Arizona, but after only two All-American seasons, he impulsively dropped out to enlist in the Marines, succumbing to a lingering case of wanderlust and setting a precedent for a fundamental character flaw—the inability to carry through with anything. He ended up serving two tours at Subic Bay, and then returned to Tempe with a Filipina wife, Lita Bautista. After some pro-ams and local tournaments, Davis went pro, and he did fairly well, enough to make a living, at least. He started off with mini-tours like the Space Coast, then progressed to the old Ben Hogan minor-league tour, where he had two wins, but it took him four trips to Q School, the annual three-stage qualifying tournament, before he was able to get his P.G.A. card. Even with his card, though, the P.G.A. Tour proved brutal: he would miss cuts and not finish in the money, leaving him with nothing to cover his expenses. He did better each year, collecting a handful of top-ten finishes, and he had phenomenal success overseas on the Asian and South American tours, three wins and several seconds in Korea, Malaysia, Singapore, Japan, and Argentina. But Davis wasn't satisfied. He had expected to be a star, not a journeyman. He wanted a P.G.A. victory.

The closest he got was at the Western Open in Chicago one year, when Patrick was nine. Because of rain delays, the field was forced to play thirty-six holes on the final day—a lucky convergence of events, as it happened, since Davis fell into a groove. He started the fourth round one shot behind the lead, was grouped with Freddie Couples and Tom Watson, and ripped through the front nine. At the turn, the leaderboard had him three ahead. Sitting at home in Tempe, Lita and Patrick watched Davis on national television. They knew what a victory would mean: a two-year exemption from qualifying, appearance fees, big bucks for clinics and endorsements. But it began to rain on the course again, and on the fourteenth, Davis sliced his drive into a fairway bunker, the ball rolling into a tiny puddle of casual water. He was allowed to take a drop, but he tanked his second shot anyway and was lucky to bogey the hole. After that, he unraveled. He had a natural draw to his swing, right to left, but suddenly everything was going on a fade, slicing to the right. So he did the worst thing a golfer, any athlete, could do: he started thinking. He began adjusting his stance, his hands, trying to *change* what had taken years to get steady and automatic. He finished five strokes behind Tom Watson, came in fourth in the tournament. The following year, he lost his P.G.A. card, and then regularly had to attend Q School again because he wouldn't be among the top 125 money winners at the end of the season. Soon, he was relegated once more to the minor leagues.

Lita was lonely. Davis would be on the road for thirty-five consecutive weeks, and even if she had the opportunity, she never went to tournaments with him anymore. She had Patrick and Brian, and she felt snubbed by the other Tour wives, with their blond hair and cheerleader smiles. Patrick would come home from school and see her lying in a chaise longue chair in their backyard, sunbathing in the dry heat. She had no friends, nothing to occupy her. For a while, she pretended—for Patrick's sake—to share his passion for air shows, and they chased across the Southwest to attend acrobatic flying performances, especially by the Blue Angels and the Thunderbirds, but the driving quickly wore on her, and she fell back into a listless gloom.

When her mother became ill, Lita returned to the Philippines. She kept extending her trip, saying it'd only be another week. Finally, Patrick talked to her on the telephone and asked, "When are you coming back?"

"I don't think I come back, Patrick," she said. "There I have no life."

"What about me and Brian?"

"Maybe soon," she said, sobbing, "I visit?"

Davis took a job as the club pro at the Del Monte Golf Course in San Vicente and bought the house in Rosarita Bay, and he thought he could raise his boys while still competing in one tournament a month, dropping them off with sundry baby-sitters so he could play on the Nike Tour or the Powerbilt Tour or the Hooters Tour. He brought back gifts, souvenirs: cowboy hats, clothing with the insignia of practically every baseball and football team, model planes, a kitten, a sheepskin toilet seat cover, an inflatable pool, and, incredibly one month, the seaplane—a hulking, ghostly piece of junk, stripped of everything salvageable.

The boys, who were so young then, began fighting over the souvenirs. During one of their arguments, Brian took the aluminum bat Davis had just given to them and smashed

Patrick's favorite model Corsair. Thereafter, Davis gave them identical pairs of everything, but the situation did not improve, exacerbated by a succession of taffy-brained young girlfriends who needed more mothering than the boys. Brian was doing badly in school, and Patrick nagged his father about money, about responsibility. Davis finally acceded to the inevitable. He retired from competitive golf, stuck to his job as the club pro, teaching hackers, and made a faithful, pathetic attempt at fatherhood.

▪   ▪   ▪

JULIE Fulcher filed a petition for Brian to become a dependent of the court, under Section 300 of the California Welfare and Institution Code.

Without being asked, Brian dressed up for the hearing, changing into a white oxford shirt, gray slacks, and black shoes—his band recital outfit. As they waited for Becklund to give them a ride to the courthouse in San Vicente, Brian inspected Patrick's face. "Did you shave?" he asked.

"Yeah."

"It doesn't look like you shaved."

"Trust me. I did."

Brian continued to stare at him. "You always look tired," he said.

At the hearing in Juvenile Court, after some preliminaries, Fulcher presented a report. "Brian is experiencing intense feelings of rejection and abandonment from his father's absence and his brother's impending departure, compounded by his mother's prior relocation to the Philippines. While there are no findings of physical, sexual, or substance abuse

in the home, Brian is clearly suffering severe emotional damage in the form of depression and withdrawal. He has developed self-destructive tendencies and is now a danger to
himself, indicated by the self-inflicted wound to his head.

"His father, who left his children without adequate provi-
sions for their support or supervision, cannot be reached. He
has demonstrated a history of neglect and irresponsibility,
and he is currently insolvent. Brian's brother, Patrick, has
been the psychological parent in the family. He is exception-
ally bright, but the lack of stable adult role models in his life
has made him angry and oppositional. He is contemptuous
with regard to authority figures and was uncooperative during the investigative phase. There is also some question about
the veracity of his statements, as to the circumstances under
which his father left and his current whereabouts."

The judge, who had been wearily paging through the case
file, abruptly stood up. She was forty or so, and she had a
weird, wide streak of gray in her hair, which was bunned.
Underneath her robe, Patrick now saw, she wore jeans. She
reached over to the bailiff and asked for a box of Kleenex,
blew her nose, then sat down again. "What about this,
Patrick?" she said in a faint Texan accent. "Are you telling
the whole truth? Is your father coming home any day now, or
should we file a missing persons report?"

Nonplussed, Patrick didn't respond. Beckland had warned
him on the ride to San Vicente that this judge was unconven-
tional, that she didn't talk like other judges. She had a nickname—"the cowgirl judge."

"Gene, any clue?" the judge asked.

"No," Becklund said. "I've called every golf tour in the

country, and nothing. I can't even figure out how he's traveling. He left his car behind, but he hasn't charged anything
like rentals or airline tickets or motels on his credit cards."

"Should I finish reading the petition?" Fulcher asked.

"Patrick," the judge said, ignoring Fulcher, "do you know
where your father is? Is he really playing golf somewhere, or
did he just take off on you?"

Patrick flushed, feeling all eyes on him.

"I know that your instinct is to protect your brother and
your father both," the judge said, "but the position of this
court is that it's always best, whenever possible, to preserve
the family. What that means is we're not going to chuck Brian
into some group home or youth authority, and we're not
going to toss your father—if he ever comes back—in jail, no
matter how much of a bum he's been. We're going to give
him all the help he needs so he and Brian can stay together.
We'll give him child care, housekeeping assistance, parent
education classes, financial aid—"

"We're not poor," Patrick said. "We're middle-class."

"Ah, he speaks," the judge said. "So this is the deal, young
man: if your father's on some extended postadolescent junket
and eventually he comes to his senses and waddles back con-
trite, we'll reunite him with Brian, which is what we all
want—the happy ending. But if he straight out abandoned
you, and he had every reason to, with his debts and with you,
his trusty, reliable slave, going off to the Naval Academy, we
have to think about something more permanent. It's hard
enough placing an eleven-year-old boy in foster care. Long-
term is even more difficult. I know you don't want to hear
this, Brian, but the best thing for you then would be some-

thing like Fost-Adopt, a fast track to adoption. The last thing
we want is for you to be bounced from home to home, year
after year."

Patrick turned to Brian, whose face was slick with tears.
"Where's Dad?" Brian whispered to his brother. "Do you
know?"

"He's not in the United States," Patrick finally admitted.
"He said he was going to Malaysia to join the Asian Tour,
and he'd be back in October."

"Has he called you since he left?" the judge asked.

"No."

"Do you believe he'll be back in October?"

"I don't know," Patrick said.

"What did he think would happen to Brian in the mean-
time?"

"I don't know," Patrick lied.

▪ ▪ ▪

IT was in February. Patrick had been doing the bills and
couldn't find the calculator. He opened a drawer in his
father's bureau and discovered a stack of papers: eligibility
requirements for P.G.A. and Nike events, information about
the Australian, South American, Asian, and European tours,
an application for the upcoming Q School.

Patrick confronted his father, who was outside, washing
his vintage Corvette in the driveway. "Are you thinking
about playing full-time again?" he asked Davis. "Is that what
you've been doing on these trips? Playing in tournaments?"

"I didn't want to tell you until I was sure."

"You can't."

"I've got someone who's willing to bankroll me for a year."

"You can't. You can't do it."

"Stop saying that. Something's different about my swing. It's liquid, it just flows. I heard someone call it true gravity once. You take back your club, and you just *know* where it's going to fall. You don't even have to try. It's almost embarrassing, how easy it is. Have you ever had that feeling?"

"Dad, I'm leaving for the academy in June."

"Just a year," Davis said. "Give me a year. I'll go overseas and fine-tune, and then I'll get my card back in October."

"What're you talking about, overseas?"

"I'm never going to make it here nonexempt. It's bullshit trying to enter these pissant tournaments by Monday qualifying. I'm playing hot, but I don't get practice rounds, I don't know the courses, there's just no way I'll get tournament-ready like this. But with my wins and career earnings, I get a free pass into any event on the Asian Tour."

"What will Brian do? He can't live here by himself."

"You could defer going to Annapolis. Couldn't you do that?" His father put both hands on Patrick's shoulders. "Listen, this is it for me. I don't want to regret not trying. I might as well be dead if I don't try."

"What about me?" Patrick said. He thought of his youth, the burdens of domestic duties and part-time jobs, every minute taken up caring for Brian or working, the flying lessons and girlfriends he'd never had. How many times had he pictured the runway at Pensacola, shimmering in the Florida heat as he sped down it in an F-18? "You can't keep doing this," he told his father. "What if by some miracle you get your card back? Then what? Will you ask for another year? You have to stop this. You have to grow up."

Davis pushed Patrick, who tripped and fell to the ground. "Don't give me that shit," Davis said. "I raised you and Brian myself all these years. You think that didn't take sacrifice? I gave up my P.G.A. career for you, and now I'm asking you for one lousy fucking year. You've got nothing but time, but you can't wait to bail out of here. You're the one who wants to abandon this family, not me."

HOW was it, Patrick wondered, that they had no relatives? How was it that not just one, but both of their parents had deserted them?

The judge deemed Brian a dependent child of the court. He would be allowed to stay with Patrick until the end of the month, while Julie Fulcher tried to find a suitable foster home for him. In six months, if Davis did not return, his parental rights would be severed, and Brian would be placed permanently in long-term foster care or guardianship or adoption.

Over the next week, Fulcher took Brian and Patrick to visit two possible foster families. The first was "race-specific," a Filipino couple with a squalling baby girl. They barely spoke English. The second couple—white—had two teenage foster children and two kids of their own—also white. The woman kept asking if there would be any special dispensations if they decided to take Brian. Did he have a learning disability? Attention deficit disorder? "Well," she said, "we'll still get extra because he's a boy, am I right?"

Throughout these visits and later at home, Brian was stonily stoic. Patrick had quit his job at Clothilde's Bistro to spend all his remaining time with him, but his brother hardly spoke to him. One afternoon, Patrick suggested they go fishing, and Brian obligingly loaded the boat with him, making spitting sounds through pressed lips. But when Patrick couldn't get the Evinrude motor to turn over, Brian took off his life preserver, stowed it underneath the bench, and walked off without a word, Patrick calling after him, "Wait, I'll fix it. Hey, just give me a minute."

Over dinner that night, Patrick asked, "Do you want to talk?" and Brian said, "What's there to talk about?" and finished his meal.

▪   ▪   ▪

AT the end of the week, Ms. Fulcher drove up to the house, bringing Evelyn Yung with her. "Brian's at Billy Kim's," Patrick said, confused by Miss Yung's presence.

"That's okay," Fulcher told him. "Can we sit?"

In the living room, the two women sat together on the sofa, Patrick opposite them in an armchair. "There's something the judge didn't discuss, another possibility for Brian," Fulcher said.

"What?"

"There's a program called kinship care. If you really want to stay in Rosarita Bay, with Brian, you could. With court supervision and A.F.D.C., you could be his custodian."

"I'm not eighteen yet."

"You're close enough. We could get a special disposition."

"The judge would agree to that?"

"I think she would," Fulcher said. "I'll be honest with you, Patrick. I don't think it's such a hot idea, but I thought you should at least have the option. It's not your problem with authority, anything like that, I'm worried about. It's that if you stayed, you'd never get over all the things you could've done—the Academy, being a pilot, all your dreams. It's too much to give up, and you'd never forgive yourself, and then you'd blame your brother. What kind of life could you and Brian have, anyway?"

"Is this something you want to think about?" asked Miss Yung. "Do you want to stay with Brian?"

Patrick felt himself constricting—his throat, his lungs. Was this what Davis and Lita had felt, internal organs choking with guilt because they had wanted, more than anything, to escape? Could Brian sense that what Patrick had feared most was being forced to stay with him, and did he hate him for it, hate him so much he had pounded his head into a desk, disgusted that Patrick was no different than their mother and father? "Don't make me decide this," Patrick said. "I can't decide this."

"Then would you let Brian stay with me?" Miss Yung asked. "As his guardian?"

"You'd be willing to do that?"

"I'd like to," she said. "I'd like to very much. It's not an entirely selfless gesture. I have no one, Patrick. I don't know how it happened, but somehow I've ended up alone, and I've begun to accept that maybe I'll always be alone. It'd be nice, for a change, to think about someone other than myself."

"Did you have an affair with Becklund?"

"Patrick," Fulcher said.

"You broke up his family. Did you think about them? His three kids?"

"I did," Miss Yung said. "They're all I could think about. They're why I ended it. They're why I told him to go back to his wife."

Patrick was silent for a long minute. Miss Yung was wearing a skirt, and he stared at a scar on her knee. It looked like an old injury, from childhood, but he had never noticed it before, although he thought he had, over the years, memorized every bit of her. "Will you buy him a trumpet?"

"Excuse me?"

"He's always worried he'll lose his embouchure because he doesn't have his own trumpet and he can't practice enough. It doesn't have to be new. A used one would be okay."

Miss Yung nodded. "I think I could manage that."

▪   ▪   ▪

USUALLY on Saturdays, Patrick didn't get home until past one, but there had been a power outage at the restaurant that night—a tree knocking down a line—and if it had not been for this random intervention of nature, he wouldn't have caught his father in the act of abandoning them. Patrick had been dismissed early, and as he drove up to the house, he saw a new Lexus Coupe beside it, the engine running. He peered at the person sitting in the driver's seat of the car—an outline of a face, a pretty Asian woman—and for a second, he had thought that it was his mother. Davis emerged from the house then, struggling with a suitcase and two golf bags. They had stared at each other, Davis's breath hurried, clouding in the cold. There had been no mistake about his intent: Brian was sleeping over at Billy Kim's, and Patrick hadn't been due home for hours. "I'll be back in October," Davis had said. "I'll come back to the States for Q School in October."

"You bastard."

"I left five thousand dollars for you. I'll try to wire more from Kuala Lumpur. If you need to, sell the Corvette."

Patrick had thought of his mother then, buying a ticket with an open return date, promising to be on the first plane home as soon as her mother was well. "You're not coming back, are you?"

"I will. I swear to you, I will."

"Goddamn you!" Patrick had screamed. He had grabbed Davis and shoved him against the side of the house. "You're dead to me. You don't exist. You're dead," he had whispered, and then he had let him go.

■   ■   ■

ON their last full day together, Patrick and Brian went to the aquarium in Monterey.

Brian had taken the news about Miss Yung's offer with little comment at first, merely allowing that he wouldn't mind living with her, but he didn't have to say much to communicate his relief.

After the aquarium, the boys drove to the beach at Rummy Creek and piled logs of driftwood into a fortress, letting them bake in the sun, protected from the wind. They watched the windsurfers for an hour, then both needed to pee. They stole away behind the rocks and pissed side by side. Brian glanced at Patrick, then at himself. "When am I going to get some pubes on my pecker?" he asked.

At home, they packed his things. Patrick wasn't leaving for the Academy for another few days, but Julie Fulcher had recommended Brian move to Miss Yung's early. He could get used to sleeping in his new bed while Patrick was still in town, while they could still see each other evenings. It'd be less traumatic for him, particularly since the bank was repossessing the house and Patrick had to clear it out.

Patrick made his brother's favorite meal—corned beef and boiled potatoes and cabbage, of all things. After washing the dishes, Brian held out a pair of scissors to Patrick. "You want to cut my hair now?"

Patrick wrapped a sheet around his brother's neck and began trimming hanks of hair. "Miss Yung said I could bring Lucy," Brian told him. "You want her? She's good company."

"No, you should take her. She's your cat." He pushed down Brian's ear so he could cut around it.

"He might come back, you know," Brian said.

Combing his hair, Patrick said, "You shouldn't count on it."

"I know."

Patrick moved in front of Brian to clip his bangs. He carefully snipped the hair over his eyes. "I'll come visit," Patrick said.

"I know you will."

Crying, the brothers hugged each other.

■   ■   ■

PATRICK held a yard sale and sold the furniture. Afterward, he roamed through the house, collecting whatever was usable and making a stack in the corner for Goodwill to pick up. The rest he would drive to the dump. He would keep the boat and the Corvette at Miss Yung's place, but he didn't know what to do about the seaplane. He couldn't convince any scrap companies to pick it up. Nor could he decide about his father's things—the trophies and plaques, the discards of clothing and equipment—whether to store them or throw them away. He stood in his father's bedroom, looking at a couple of stray golf balls on the floor. Abstractly, Patrick remembered the hot, sweaty afternoons at the airstrip, the time he went airborne, snagged the Titleist in the webbing of his mitt.

He sat down on the carpet. He might return in October, Patrick let himself think for an instant. Bring home another pair of identical gifts. But just as quickly, Patrick knew he wouldn't. What was it that made people so weak?

He gathered all of Davis's belongings and put them in the seaplane. He dismantled the outboard motor on the Boston Whaler, cleaned out the carburetor, changed the sparks and oil, and blew clear the fuel tubes. Rigging two pulleys to the transom, he fashioned a split towline out of rope, then tied it to the seaplane. Inside the cabin, he twisted rags and stuffed them into the mouths of four gasoline cans. He stepped into the boat and started the motor, idling until the line was pulled taut, then slowly, he opened up the throttle and towed the seaplane down the canal.

He would take it out to sea, far off the coast. He would remove the drain plugs from the pontoons, pour gasoline over the cabin, and throw in a lit book of matches. Then he would run the boat some distance away and drift with the swell, watch the fire accumulate, the gas cans erupt. He would wait until the seaplane began to crumple into the water, and then he would move the boat a little closer, and watch it sink.

THE POSSIBLE HUSBAND

SOMEWHERE APPROACHING a hundred. Not an outrageous number, really. Duncan Roh had started at fourteen, and he was forty-one now, so a rather modest average of four a year. Some of them had been *haoles*—whites—but most had been Asian amazons like Sunny Foo, his current lover, who tended to walk with her pelvis a little ahead of her, long, lazy steps seeming to drift too wide.

Sunny Foo was his restaurant designer. For unknown and regrettable reasons, Duncan—recently retired, with enough cash to pursue the sole thing he'd ever been committed to, big-wave surfing, full time—had decided to open a sushi restaurant in Rosarita Bay. He wanted to name it Banzai Pipeline, after the famous break on the North Shore of Oahu, where he had grown up. His idea for decor had been a couple of surfboards on the walls and a big-screen TV playing surf videos. But Sunny had other ideas, very expensive, out-landish ideas, like double-molded Plexiglas canopied over the length of the sushi bar, pumped with rushing water, sculpted to resemble a perfect, hollow Pipeline barrel just before it tubed.

Sunny argued that diners wanted restaurants to be *theater,* to be an *event,* but Duncan said no, absolutely not. The restaurant was supposed to take six months to build and cost a quarter of a million dollars. Now it was eight months and pushing 400K. They got into screaming rows, obscenity-laden tirades. Then, naturally, they started fucking. And, nat-urally, Duncan found himself relenting: well, if we really have to have those tiny scallop-shaped sconces, and they're two hundred bucks apiece, okay. With Sunny, sex and manipula-tion seemed conjoined. Whenever a new section was installed or finished in the restaurant, she wanted to fuck there, as if to christen her conquest.

This Friday, it was the patined copper walls, rippling with water that cascaded from ceiling to floor—a compromise on the original wave concept. Lit by recessed lamps, the walls reflected a flickering amber and green warmth, reminding Duncan of mornings of his youth, sitting on his surfboard, lifted up and down by rills as the sun broke over the horizon. He had to admit that the walls were beautiful.

"You see?" Sunny said. "I *do* know what I'm doing." She kicked a curled shard of copper sheet that was lying on the still-unfinished floor. The work crew had left quickly for the weekend, dropping tools and materials on the spot, and Duncan navigated around nail guns and circular saws and tubs of joint compound as he followed Sunny to the far wall, against which she stood, palms flush on the slick metal, as if waiting to be frisked, miniskirt scooched over her bum.

At Duncan's house on Skyview Ridge Road, they put Sunny's clothes in the dryer and took a hot bath together. "Are you ever going to get some furniture for this place?" she asked. Most of the house—bought three years ago, a three-story cedar-and-glass behemoth with wraparound decks—was empty.

"One of these days."

"You could let me decorate it for you."

"Thanks, but you're bankrupting me enough," Duncan said. "Besides, I don't trust your tastes. Everything has to be a theme park."

Her own high-rise condo in San Francisco looked like an industrial machine shop, an amalgam of sleek steel and chrome. Her bed was the centerpiece—a frightening apparatus with iron-beam posts extending upward to intersect at a hulking block and tackle, thick chains dangling over the sheets. Duncan couldn't imagine sleeping underneath the contraption—not that he would ever be invited. Sunny had imposed strict ground rules: they didn't spend the night, they didn't go on "dates," they didn't chat on the phone, they just fucked. They got together on Tuesday and Friday nights, and had no ownership over the rest of the week.

In the tub, Sunny drew her knees apart and grasped his penis between the arches of her feet.

"That's not going to do anything," Duncan told her.

"No?" she said. "Come on, giddyup."

"I'm not nineteen," he said. "I need a little more time to reload."

"I thought Korean men were so virile. The view alone deserves a salute."

The view was pretty good: she was especially tall and long-limbed for a Chinese woman, and she had candied proportions, large areolas on her breasts, hairless and pink down there, too. "Sunny, how many people have you slept with?"

"Men or women?"

"*Ho brah,*" Duncan said. At his parents' house in Haleiwa, they had spoken a mix of English, Korean, and Hawaiian Pidgin.

"I've kind of lost count, if you want to know the truth," Sunny said. "But I can tell you exactly how many animals."

She was kidding, wasn't she? Although there was that block and tackle above her bed, and her dog, a big, muscular Rhodesian Ridgeback named Foo Man Stud, seemed unusually attached to her, snarling and lunging at Duncan whenever he saw him, restrained from tearing him apart only by his choke chain, which Sunny would yank mercilessly, laughing. Sunny used to like choking Duncan, too, sliding her hand from his chest to his throat as they made love, until he asked her to stop.

He looked at Sunny, who was scooping bathwater over her breasts. She smiled at him, then slipped the tip of her tongue out and set it aflutter in a reptilian blur.

"You're a piece of work, aren't you?" he said.

"You don't know the half of it."

Maybe she was into asphyxiophilia, a host of other depravities. He didn't want to know. Sex at this point in his life was more interesting in theory than in practice, and, more and more, this arrangement with Sunny was becoming too weird, too impersonal for him, as if he were there purely to service and amuse her.

"Sunny," he said, "I don't think we should see each other anymore."

She raised an eyebrow. "No?"

"No. If you want, you can keep working on the restaurant."

"Well, *duh,*" she said. "Otherwise I'd sue your ass for sexual harassment."

She got out of the tub and slowly toweled herself dry and began combing her hair.

"You don't want to know why?" he asked.

"Why you're dumping me?"

He nodded.

"Oh, it's probably I'm too independent for you, I can't give you a commitment, I'm not subservient enough, I just want you for sex, I'm a ball-buster, a bitch, a slut, what do you know, just like a man. Nothing I haven't heard before. It's pathetic how easily intimidated Asian men are."

S P R I N G

ESTHER Miyabe didn't like sex much, which, after Sunny, didn't really bother Duncan. They met at the grand opening of Banzai Pipeline, introduced to each other by a former colleague of Duncan's from Summit Strategy, the venture capital firm on Sand Hill Road where he had made his killing.

Esther, a fourth-generation Japanese American, was impressed with Duncan's restaurant, and with his money, and with his house, which he allowed her to furnish and decorate

in tasteful country casual. Esther owned a nice Victorian herself in Pacific Heights, where he was supposed to be at four
o'clock. She had invited over a group of scientists from her
biotech lab, Genetein, to watch the semifinals of the
N.C.A.A. basketball tournament. All week, though, Duncan
had been tracking satellite images, wave models, and buoy
reports, and he knew a good-sized swell would be arriving at
Rummy Creek with the outgoing tide.

"It might be the last swell of the season," he told Esther on
the phone in the morning.

"Fine," she said.

"I'll be there by six, in plenty of time for the second game."

"You do what you have to do. You think surfing's more
important, you go ahead," she said.

"Come on, Esther. It's just the Final Four. You don't even
like basketball."

"You don't understand anything, do you?" she said.

He had tried, but he couldn't explain Rummy Creek to her.
It was an aberration, a freak of nature. There weren't supposed to be any big-wave breaks in Rosarita Bay, where the
main stretch of shoreline, Pismo Beach, offered only mushy,
waist-high dribblers. Rummy Creek? It was way off the highway, hidden behind the Air Force radar station. Some windsurfers knew about it, launching off an occasional ramp on
the inside break, but on the outside, even during a fat ten-
foot swell, it barely capped over. No one ever thought to surf
Rummy Creek until Duncan Roh twelve years ago.

He lived in San Francisco then, still working as an investment analyst. On a January day, his regular spot, Ocean
Beach, had been blown out by an onshore gale, and he drove

down the coast to explore, glimpsed the radar dish, and hiked down to it. His father, an Army civilian, supervised radar installations in Hawaii, and Duncan thought he'd be curious about what was there. Before he crested the headlands, he could hear and feel it—the concussive detonation of an enormous wave breaking. As he came over the rise, he was stunned to see that the reef was at least half a mile out. Sets of waves smoked in and humped up into towering gray-green peaks, pitched out, boomed, and peeled left and right, foam roiling.

Over the next week, Duncan figured out the topography of the outer reef. It sat twenty-five feet below the surface, shoaling abruptly out of deep water, which explained why it usually lay inert. About thirty days each winter, however, groundswells generated by Aleutian storms pumped unimpeded across open ocean, and the first thing they hit after two thousand miles was Rummy Creek, causing waves to jack up into grinding, monster barrels big enough to enclose a bus.

It took Duncan a month to work up the nerve to attempt a ride. He chose a smallish fifteen-footer, stroking hard to get up to speed, hopping on his feet. He thought he had taken off safely on the shoulder, but the wave surged upward, forcing him to drop steeply down its face. He landed, wobbled, regained his balance, and leaned hard to carve back up the wall, then screamed down the line, shooting across two hundred yards before the whitewater caught up to him and blasted him off his board—the ride of his life.

He became obsessed with Rummy Creek, and surfed it alone for the next seven years. At first he had wanted to keep the place to himself, but when he finally told a few surfers about it, no one would paddle out with him. It was too scary, too dangerous. The water was fifty degrees, and even with a neoprene wetsuit, hood, gloves, and booties, hypothermia could set in quickly, making you too disoriented to survive a hold-down, which was unavoidable at Rummy Creek. The waves were so big, so fast, so heavy, they created their own wind. When they broke, they registered on seismographs at Berkeley. As you skittered across the ambient chop on the face, the waves were relentless, chasing after you like an avalanche, an imploding building, a malevolent Niagara, and if you fell and got sucked over the falls, they would drive you deep to the bottom, which was rutted with sharp crevices and caves. Down there, the turbulence aerated the water, not dense enough to swim. For half a minute, you were stuck in a punishing, mauling spin cycle, your eardrums close to rupturing from the pressure, and if you were lucky enough to claw to the surface, you were still in the impact zone, another wave about to dump on you, or, almost as unpleasantly, you were pulled by the current and pummeled against the jagged rocks on the inside, which would cut you up nicely for the great white sharks that prowled the shore and sometimes left carcasses of sea lions on the beach, organs and muscle and bone hanging out of missing bellies.

Yet, gradually, Tank, JuJu, and Skunk B. joined Duncan at Rummy Creek (they called him DooRow). They were young turks from Santa Cruz with bleached cornrows and tattoos and pierced tongues, all soul surfers, purists who shunned contests and fame. They did everything they could to keep this gnarly, mysto spot secret, vibing out any Barneys who came over the hill, Tank keying their cars and snapping antennas. Even the townspeople cooperated. They all knew about the place, but if a stranger slunk into Rosarita Bay and asked about the location of a big-wave break, they'd deny its existence.

Word would leak out eventually, Duncan knew. Some photographer from a surf magazine would capture Rummy Creek on a good day, and instantly it'd be all over, world-famous overnight, just like the North Shore. Then there'd be a hundred punks on the water, six yahoos vying for each wave, and Duncan would be crowded off this reef he'd discovered, this primeval place that inspired and terrorized his every waking moment.

Everywhere else, he was merely an average surfer, not close to being a professional. Particularly on small waves, while pre-pubescent kids were ripping out aerials and snapbacks, Duncan looked like a novice. But on big waves, he excelled, and he was at his best at Rummy Creek. It was where Duncan felt the most alive. He didn't have time to think about anything except the pitch and shape of each wave. He wasn't obliged to anyone who could get in his way or disappoint him. He was attuned to every dip and yaw of his board, sentient to a world ablaze in iridescent color: the bottle-green of the water, the spindrift floating across the air, the magenta sky underneath black storm clouds, the patches of mustard bursting on the hills. He was out there on the terrible sea, and it was pointless and deadly, what he was doing, and it was beautiful.

He got to Esther's house at eight-thirty.

"Why didn't you at least change?" Esther said. "And what the hell happened to your leg?"

"Just a scratch," he said.

His hair was stiff with salt, and he was wearing his usual

après-surf apparel: fleece vest, T-shirt, shorts, and sheepskin Ugg boots. The swell hadn't quite lived up to billing, a little lumpy and small, but he had managed to snag some decent rides, not falling until the end of the day, when he got careless taking off on a wave and was crunched, hitting the bottom and gashing his shin through his wetsuit.

The cut was simple to fix—seven stitches and several feet of gauze—but the doctor at the clinic had been concerned about his shoulder, which she thought he might have separated, and had made him wait for an X ray.

"The second game still on?" he asked Esther. He caught the last few minutes of the blowout, ate some of the sushi he'd had delivered from Banzai, and tried to chitchat with Esther's coworkers from Genetein. Most, like her, were crystallographers, an occupation in the pharmaceutical industry that Duncan didn't fully understand, no matter how often Esther had tried to educate him. Something to do with growing protein crystals and studying the three-dimensional molecular structures of potential drugs, hopefully billion-dollar drugs.

The conversation at these parties always excluded Duncan, the talk revolving around science (cytosolic phospholipase A_2?), research publications, conferences, and political maneuvers for promotions. The only topic he could have participated in didn't interest him much anymore: money. These Genetein scientists were cash-rich from a merger with Pfizer a few years back, and they all wanted to discuss stocks and I.P.O.s with Duncan, but, insisting he was retired, he politely recused himself.

"You couldn't give them a nibble?" Esther said as they undressed for bed.

"I wasn't being evasive. I'm totally out of the loop since I quit."

"People think you're weird," she said.

"Why?"

"Because you don't do anything but surf."

"I have the restaurant."

"You have a manager running it. You're not even there most nights."

"I like my life," Duncan said, lying on the bed. "I worked very hard to get this life."

"So you could regress into a Hawaiian slacker?" She flashed him a *shaka* with her hand, thumb and pinkie extended out. "Aloha, dude," she said mockingly.

Duncan laughed. She was cute. "You know there's more to me than that," he said.

"Is there? What are you going to do when you're too old to surf?" Esther wiped a tissue over her Mary Janes, then went to the closet and placed the shoes on her tiered rack, nudging them until they were straight and equidistant from the other pairs. When she came back to the bed, she was crying a little.

"Hey," Duncan said softly. "What's wrong?"

"I've invested so much in this relationship," Esther said, "and I'm beginning to think it's not going to work."

S U M M E R

HE met Ariel Belieu, Rosarita Bay's reference librarian, in a meditation class, which he joined sensing Esther might have been prophetic: perhaps his surfing days were numbered. He had herniated a disk in his final session at Rummy Creek in the spring, to add to his collection of four broken ribs, a lung contusion, a fractured forearm, and a dislocated knee. He was logging more hours at the chiropractor's, and his doctor had told him he was showing signs of osteoporosis.

Duncan hoped meditation would help him focus, keep him sharp enough to avoid bad falls. In the class, he developed a visualization ritual—a succession of images that arose unbidden. He saw himself in a clearing of a tropical forest, standing underneath an outdoor shower, and he inhaled as he lifted the shower's pump lever, exhaled as he pushed it down, water streaming down his hair, his back, lifted and pushed the lever twice more, inhaling, exhaling. Then he walked down a path through the trees, his feet suctioning off the wet, gray clay, until he broke through the lush leafage to a wide mesa of brilliant yellow, dry grass that sloped down to the ocean, where rows of flawless A-frame peaks were breaking, crests feathering in the wind. At the cliff's edge was a swimming pool, and he dove into it, gliding down and parking himself peacefully on the bottom, looking up at the wavering surface, and then he emerged and sat in a white Adirondack chair, everything now irradiated in a kaleidoscope of colors, a wonderful phantasmagoria that eventually contracted into a sphere of glowing orange amid darkness, a warm, hovering spot of light.

It was elusive, that transcendent spot of light. He couldn't get there very often. His meditation teacher told him it was called a *thigle* in Tibetan and a *bindhu* in Sanskrit, and she was amazed that he had seen it at all, particularly in the first week of class. It was a stage reserved for advanced practitioners.

Ariel never saw the *thigle,* and soon she quit meditating altogether. She had signed up for the class to combat stress, a common and severe affliction among reference librarians, Duncan was surprised to learn. Too many stupid questions from stupid patrons who turned abusive when an answer wasn't forthcoming.

He made up a goofy routine—Funk & Wagnalls. Whenever he picked her up, as he did this Thursday for dinner, he asked, "What the Funk?" The dumbest request of the day.

"A high school girl wanted photographs of the Underground Railroad."

Duncan was slow on the take, but then laughed uproariously. "Okay," he said, "Wagnalls?" An intriguing nugget of referential miscellany.

"Sharks are the only intrauterine cannibals in the world," Ariel said. "The fetuses prey on each other in the womb until just one remains."

"Ugh," Duncan said. "Sharks. I hate even thinking about them."

They decided to go to Clothilde's Bistro, both a little tired of sushi and teriyaki by this point. Clothilde's was modeled after a French country bistro with dark paneling and chairs upholstered in red velvet, and it was one of Ariel's favorite places to eat. "Food from the homeland," she said, though she was from Indiana. Still, she was ethnically French-Jewish, with brooding Gallic features, and she was an epicurean snob. She had been aghast when she'd discovered Duncan making a fried Spam sandwich for lunch one day. Spam was beloved in Hawaii. Locals bought Spam by the case. "Gross," Ariel had said.

"When you grow up with it, it's kind of comforting," he had told her.

His childhood was of intense interest to Ariel, because hers had been miserable, and he claimed that his had been anything but. He couldn't recall, in fact, being depressed at any time in his life. She was appalled. She didn't believe him. Denial, she declared. There had to be some reason he had never married, never lived with anyone, never lasted more than ten months in any relationship. So she began an inquisition, questioning him about his family in Hawaii, subjecting him to hours of probing, like coerced psychodynamic therapy sessions that left him exhausted and demoralized.

A couple of nights ago, though, Ariel thought she had stumbled onto a clue, a tantalizing glimmer of bleakness, a *thigle* of pain deep within his oppressive aura of beatitude. She had asked him when he had cried last, and, after pondering, he remembered crying—quite a bit, actually—when he was twelve. For a year his father had been assigned to Yongsan Eighth Army Base in Seoul, Korea. It was the only time in Duncan's life since he was a six-year-old grommet that he would not surf at least twice a week.

"Tell me what you remember about Korea," Ariel said.

As they ate in Clothilde's, he told her what he could remember.

He remembered meeting Korean relatives he couldn't communicate with, and their poverty. He remembered traditional Han-bok clothes, so colorful, and trekking through muddy hills to visit the graves of nameless ancestors. He remembered Quonset huts painted in uniform pastels of blue, green, and yellow on the base, and G.I.s with M-16s, and military parades on Knight Field with howitzers firing off twenty-one-gun salutes.

"Go on," Ariel said to him, excited. "What else?"

He remembered an air show, the Blue Angels in their Phantom F-4s flying acrobatic stunts over Collier Field House. For the finale, they had buzzed the Han River—dry at the time, and a stone's throw from the base—and dropped napalm onto the sandbars, terrific billows of flames rising into the air. He had been thrilled by the show, but also disturbed, not understanding why until later: the arrogance of the demonstration, dropping live bombs during peacetime into the river of a foreign capital, merely to entertain the troops.

He remembered, too, going to the barber shop on Main Post, and his father ordering "the works" for him: shampoo, haircut, facial, massage. After a man trimmed his hair, a young Korean woman, one of a gaggle standing by in extremely tight, extremely short blue dresses, reclined the chair so he was lying flat, and slathered a green mineral mask on him. She returned a few minutes later to wipe it off, then wrapped a hot towel over his face and discreetly laid a thicker, larger towel over his hips. The woman took a seat on the side of the barber chair and squeezed her ass against his arm and bumped her breasts against his chest as she reached across him. From this stationary, awkward position, she massaged Duncan for ten minutes, and he got an erection, despite the shame he felt for himself and the woman, despite the eddy of rage that had swirled in him all year. He had hated not being able to surf, but more than that he had hated the *haole* Army culture.

"Is that why you go out with Asian women more than whites?" Ariel asked.

"I don't know. Maybe. I haven't really given it much thought."

"And what made you obsessed with making money?"

"I don't know about that," he said.

"Have you ever thought surfing might be a form of escapism for you? Maybe even a death wish?"

"Ariel," Duncan said, "everything doesn't have to have meaning."

"Not everything, but some things do. What worries me is you've done so little work on yourself. You won't even acknowledge you've got issues. Those stories about Korea—they're textbook. You don't think they have a little something to do with the way you describe surfing as 'soaring' and waves as 'bombs'? With your objectification of women? Duncan, don't you realize? You're a basket case."

"Ariel," Duncan said, laughing, "sometimes the past is just the past."

She raked the tines of her fork across her crème brûlée. "You know, Duncan," she said, "unless you can develop some self-awareness, we're definitely not going to make it."

F A L L

"YOU'RE late," Lily Kim told him at Beryl's Bookstore & Café. "You're always late. Why is that, when you have no responsibilities?"

This was the cantankerous Korean woman he was beginning to fall for, but who would not have him—yet. Lily Kim and Duncan were not "dating," though they had seen each other a dozen times in the last few months. They were "friends," meaning they chatted on the phone, they went out for coffee, they saw movies, they took walks, they swam laps together at the Y.M.C.A. pool, they hung out at each other's homes, but they didn't sleep over, and they didn't touch, much less kiss.

"Traffic's terrible on 71," he told her.

"We never had traffic on weekends before all you high-tech yuppies moved in with your S.U.V.s."

"Nice to see you, too," he said. She was standing in the travel section, thumbing through a guidebook, swaddled in a corduroy skirt, woolen leggings, clodhopper shoes, and a barn jacket over a crewneck over a turtleneck (she got cold easily). "What are you reading?"

She flipped the guidebook around so he could see.

"Ah, Bali," he said.

Lily frowned. "You've been there, haven't you?"

"Twice. There's a break in Uluwatu that can get double-overhead."

She shoved the guidebook back into its slot on the shelf, annoyed. It seemed that whenever she showed Duncan a photograph of a beach, he had surfed it. During the summer, when Rummy Creek was flat, he was frequently on planes, chasing waves, hopping from Tahiti and Indonesia to Chile and Costa Rica.

Lily couldn't afford to travel. She was an artist who generated a lot of critical acclaim but few sales. To pay the rent, she taught painting and drawing at San Vicente University and three other colleges. As a youth, she had taken a trip to

Korea on a roots pilgrimage, and she had gone on the requisite European backpack tour and a few initial-infatuation Mexican holidays with boyfriends, but for the most part she hadn't gotten beyond driving distance of Rosarita Bay, her hometown, in years. She yearned to go someplace warm and exotic. The walls of her house were tacked with calendars and posters and photographs torn from magazines of tropical islands—quotidian tourist images of beaches and sunsets that she appropriated for her current series, *The Far & Away*. She rephotographed the seascapes and in the darkroom enlarged them into disjointed panels—square mounted grids jarringly scaled and off-focus and saturated in a lurid hue. In an interview in the *Rosarita Bay Horizon*, Lily had explained her technique was an extension of Impressionism—the fragmented brushstrokes and intense palette of colors that painters had used to capture light and movement more immediately. But the impetus for her work, she said, was largely political, a protest against the commodification of nature—banal travelogue images now more familiar, and therefore more real, to people than the actual experience of being in nature.

Duncan missed the message entirely. Lily's work didn't have an ironic effect on him at all. It viscerally and exactly conveyed his experience in the natural world. Walking by a gallery on Main Street, he saw one of her pieces—a purplish exposure of a choppy sea lapping against a pebbled beach (Java, a left point break he had surfed a couple of years back, it turned out)—and he quickly bought it, his first art purchase.

He met Lily when she came to install the piece in his

house. After she finished, he had asked her out for coffee. She had fired back, "Are you married?" then "Are you involved with someone?" then "Are you gay but don't know it?" He answered no to each question, but Lily wasn't convinced of his trustworthiness, and on their get-togethers—she was adamant about not having them described as dates—she interrogated him about his romantic proclivities, wary of his less-than-stellar track record. He tried to persuade her that, yes, he had gone out with his share of women, but he was not a womanizer. He didn't have any sort of deep-seated, oedipally induced Peter Pan complex that prevented him from engaging in a healthy, long-term commitment.

Lily was difficult to sway. She was a serial cohabitator. Thirty-nine now, she had lived with four different men since college, mostly older artists who had ended up cheating on her. She didn't have a great opinion of artists—or men. She was sick of men. All her life she had been hemmed in and held back and pushed down by them, beginning with her father, who was uncommunicative, and her brother Danny, who was intractable, and her brother Eugene, who was kindhearted but passive to a fault. If not for intercourse, she would have become a lesbian.

They sat down in the bookstore's café section and ordered cappuccinos. While Lily talked about next week's pumpkin festival on Main Street—strictly cornball, but she couldn't resist going year after year—Duncan stared at her face. He was fascinated by the light and shadows on her face in the café, the lines of her cheekbones drawn by crescent umbras, her brown-tinted hair glinting as if by static. In her studio, he had seen some of Lily's paintings—her medium before photography—and one in particular, a self-portrait, had floored him. It was composed of blacks and dark blues and grays, but somehow had seemed luminous, dripping with color, and he had wondered how she'd done it. Now, looking at her face, he had a revelation, a *thigle* visitation. Suddenly he saw what she saw.

"Lily," he said, "I have something very important to ask you."

"What?" she asked, looking terrified, as if he were about to propose.

"Teach me how to paint."

She appeared relieved, then confused, then peeved. "Take a class. Only, not one of my classes. Someone else's class."

"Give me private lessons. I'll pay you."

She grimaced. "I wish you'd stop trying to bribe me. Like wanting to buy that painting when you know it's crap."

"I love that painting."

"I don't like the implications: cash for some goods rendered, untold services implied."

"You know I'm not like that," he said. She allowed Duncan so little. She wouldn't even introduce him to her brother Eugene, who'd moved back to Rosarita Bay last month, and whose wife, Janet, had been an Army brat on Yongsan. "You don't think this will pan out, do you?" he asked Lily.

"Why would I think that?" she said. "You're the epitome of middle-aged, male-ego wish fulfillment, enamored with this image of yourself as a lone-wolf maverick. You're perpetually looking for the perfect woman, just like you're looking for the perfect wave. You're one of those guys who'd bail at the first sign of intimacy with the three-week jitters or the three-month willies. Basically, you're every woman's nightmare."

Duncan was used to these outbursts, no longer scared off by them. "Secretly you find me irresistible," he said. "Otherwise you wouldn't keep hanging out with me."

"Did I mention deluded? Megalomaniacal?"

Duncan's pager began beeping. He pulled it out, glanced at the numbers, then stowed it back in his pocket.

"What was that?" Lily asked.

"Nothing," he said. Buoy reports. Significant wave height twenty-one feet at nineteen-second intervals. A huge swell by tomorrow. The pager automatically alerted him when a buoy topped twenty. "Lily," he said, "I'm such a nice guy. I really am."

"Would the fifty women you've slept with agree?"

He had fudged a bit on the tally, which didn't seem like that much of a lie, since often he felt as if he were dating the same woman over and over again, varying only in the texture of their complaints about him. "I really tried to make every single one of those relationships work," he told Lily.

"I see," she said. "So it's not always your fault."

"Not always."

"You're a victim yourself."

"Well, kind of."

"Of circumstance."

"Sometimes, yes."

"You're never going to get it," Lily said. "Subconsciously you're doing everything you can to end up alone."

It seemed a terrible fate to Duncan. He realized that was why he had opened the restaurant. To rescue himself from one-pot meals and nights alone with videos and errands invented to get out of the house.

"There are all these women out there," Lily said, "reduced to babbling idiots because they can't find a decent man. Then they get sold into this self-indulgent therapy bullshit on the premise that there's something wrong with *them*. It's so unnecessary, because it's really quite simple. Men are pigs. Everything you say and do, it's like you're missing some higher brain functions and you're operating purely on the stem. All I hear is oink."

"So the reason you're afraid of getting involved with me," Duncan said, "it's not that I'm a surfer, or a sexist, or that I'm emotionally unavailable, or not ambitious enough, or that I'm repressed or shallow or not Korean enough— it's got nothing to do with any of that. It's just that I'm a *man*?"

Lily smiled. "Exactly."

When he reached the headlands in the morning, he saw Skunk B. pulling into an exquisite twenty-five-foot barrel. Duncan strapped on his ankle leash, waded into the shore-break, and flopped onto the ebb of some backwash, paddling the rip into the channel. Fifteen minutes later, he was at the lineup, Tank, JuJu, and Skunk B. yelling to him in elation. The sky was an adamantine blue, cirrus clouds fanning across the northern horizon, the tide was going out, and there wasn't a whiff of wind. The water was green and glassy, clean, and for four hours they took turns shredding wave after wave, the boys hooting when Duncan nailed a drop, carved the bottom for a higher line, and then flew, gliding sweet S-turns from peak to trough to peak, speeding across the bowls. It was heaven. If only he could find a way to share this sort of elemental joy with Lily.

And then Duncan got drilled. By now, there were no more lulls between sets, just one bomb after another, and it was getting truly immense. As he teetered down the crest of a beast, his board hit a bump and wheelied, and he was thrown into freefall. He smacked the water, was sucked back up the face, and catapulted. Then he was at the bottom, churning, flesh feeling like it was being peeled. His board had splintered into three pieces—somehow he had seen that, as well as a photographer on a Jet Ski in the channel—but Duncan was intact and conscious, and he waited for the turbulence to subside so he could surface. Just as he was being released, just as he sensed himself lifting, the pressure slackening, the rush and roar quieting, he felt something clamp around his leg. His leash—a fifteen-foot line of polyurethane that tied his ankle to the broken-off tail of his board—had snagged on something underwater. A second wave was about to unload on him, and he couldn't reach the Velcro strap to unfasten the leash.

Later, JuJu told him, "Dude, we were going to get the pine *box* for you," and Duncan thought that, too, as he yanked his leg up, and yanked, and yanked, trying to get free, trying not to panic. But then he found himself noticing—delirious?—how beautiful it was down there, shafts of light refracting off the boiling icy water. He could hear rocks clacking and rolling on the ocean floor, water sucking off the reef, howling, and he was thinking how much he wanted to talk to Lily right then, describe the movement of colors to her, the shifting contours and shadows, and, bedazzled, he kept staring at the cyclones of water whirling in phosphorescent blurs—like a photograph taken with the shutter open—as he ran out of air.

DOMO ARIGATO

ON THEIR second night in Tokyo, Eugene Kim and Nikki Keliher discovered a little bar called Flashbacks, nestled in an alleyway in Akasaka. No bigger than a bedroom, the entire place was made of varnished pine—walls, ceiling, floor, booths, and tables—a tiny tinderbox that was dimly lit, windowless, but homey. It was June 1978, and the bar was owned by a faux hippie who assumed at first that Eugene was Japanese. He looked Japanese, with his delicate, long face and small nose, his whitish skin and lanky arms, but in fact he was a *nisei* of another ilk, a second-generation Korean American born and raised in Rosarita Bay. Even so, the owner, Yoshi, was friendly and gracious, and encouraged the young lovers to go up anytime to his record collection and pick out albums to play. They returned to Flashbacks practically every night, sitting happily in a booth, getting tipsy on cold Sapporo beer while listening to Derek and the Dominos, the Allman Brothers, and Earth, Wind & Fire—a perfect, welcome respite from Nikki's parents.

But one night, the music abruptly stopped. A fuse or a tube in the amplifier blew out—Yoshi couldn't figure out what it was. While he frantically dismantled the stereo, the fifteen or so patrons in the bar fidgeted. Without music, the whole rhythm of the place had been thrown off, as if in the relief of lights, and some people left. "What's everyone supposed to do now? *Talk*?" Nikki said. "Poor Yoshi." Carole King's *Tapestry* had been on the turntable before the amp had fritzed, and Nikki hummed the melody to "Way Over Yonder." Quietly, she sang the first lines to Eugene, then suddenly rose and belted it out, stepping from the booth to the head of the room. She had only a fair voice, but she made up for it with verve, *into* it, swaying, eyes closed, arms outstretched, delivering a rousing, soulful performance. "You are nuts," Eugene said as she sat down amid applause and whistles. A minute later, a woman, reading the album's liner, whispered out the opening to "Will You Love Me Tomorrow?" in wobbly English, singing louder after a few cheers, and then Yoshi brought down the house with a heartfelt rendition of "A Natural Woman." Just possibly, Nikki had started a revolution. She might have been the progenitor of *karaoke*, which, after all, had originated in Japan.

"Sometimes I wonder why you're with me," Eugene told her in the bar. "You could be with any guy you want."

"'Why'?" Nikki said. "Because you can still ask a moronic question like that after two years. Because you're timid, but secretly you'd like to jump onstage and grab the mike, and you admire that I do. Because you think I'm better than I am, and you never hold anything against me, even when I'm being a complete bitch. It's also, by the way, all of it, what infuriates me about you."

They had just graduated from Stanford. In the fall, Eugene would be going to med school at U.C.L.A., and Nikki was to join him there, entering the Ph.D. program in comparative lit, after spending the summer in Japan. Her father, Brady Keliher, was C.I.A., and he and his wife, Joanna, were stationed in Tokyo. For two weeks Eugene stayed with them, and, really, he had no idea that after this trip he would not see Nikki again for close to twenty years.

He heard a couple of rumors. After Tokyo, she went to New York and got a job with a small book publisher that specialized in Asian translations. There was also something about a struggling-musician boyfriend who happened to be loaded—an heir to Standard Oil. But that was all. Eugene lost track of her. He himself wed the first woman he dated after Nikki, Janet McElroy, and had four children. They lived for many years in L.A., but eventually Eugene took a job as an oncologist at San Vicente Memorial Hospital, and they moved to Rosarita Bay, of all places—his hometown. He had worried it would be strange to go back to Rosarita Bay, but many of the people he'd known—including his parents, who had retired to Hawaii—were gone, such was the transience of modern American life, and those who had stayed didn't really remember him. He was content with his obscurity, and in general he never left the Bay Area except to go to conferences, like the annual oncologists' meeting in St. Louis, which was where he spotted Nikki after twenty years, at the airport, as he was waiting for his flight home.

The agent at the opposite gate paged for a passenger Keliher, and Eugene glanced up and saw her walking to the counter. She was wearing a tailored gabardine pantsuit, and she was trim and fit. Probably still a runner, as she was in college. What she projected was confidence—smart, no-nonsense, good at everything she did. A world-beater. Not flashy, yet big-city hip and moneyed. They were sitting in the same TWA hub, but Nikki was a continent apart from Eugene, from the middle-aged square that he had become, color the only distinctive thing about him and his wife, who was part black.

He watched Nikki for half an hour, watched her make a cell-phone call, read a newspaper, then a magazine, open her appointment book and jot down a note. She was facing away from him, so there was no need to be surreptitious. She wouldn't have recognized him, anyway. He'd grown bald and rather lumpy. The elasticity of youth and good looks in the Kim family had gone to his brother, Danny, and his sister, Lily. He debated whether to approach her, to talk to her. What would he say? Would they have anything to say to each other? He stayed in his chair, and then boarded his flight when it was called.

▪   ▪   ▪

THEY spent his final weekend in Japan at a mountain inn in Kasugo Onsen, a village known for its natural hot springs in Nagano Prefecture. They arrived late on Friday night at the *ryokan,* and Eugene was disappointed to be put, as he had been at the Kelihers' apartment, in a separate room from Nikki.

"Your parents' idea?" he asked her.

"Probably the inn's," she said. "They're very traditional here."

"This is so silly," he told her. "We're going to be living together in a couple of months."

In the room, a futon had already been laid out on the six-*tatami* floor. Set against the wall was a low lacquer table, and a scroll of calligraphy and a vase of flowers adorned a small alcove. There was a *shoji* window screen, but it, too, was purely decorative. Eugene pulled it apart, and nothing was behind it. Austere, elegant, expensive, and utterly devoid of amenities. No chairs, television, telephone, not even a bathroom, which was down the hall.

"It's going to be very lonely in here," Eugene said to Nikki.

"Oh, I think you'll survive."

"Very lonely. Want to sneak in later for a quickie?" He wrapped his arms around her waist from behind, and, kissing her neck, tried to slip his fingers under her loose blouse and through an unmended hole in her skirt, at the knob of her hip.

She slapped at his wrist. "Stop that, you goon."

"So, we have a date?"

"Oh, sure," she said. "When I have to get up in the middle of the night to pee, I'll swing by and give you a hand job."

"Can we shake on that?"

She smacked his butt.

They could joke, but something was amiss. They had not made love while in Japan, and he could blame only so much on logistics. Even in her parents' apartment at the embassy compound, where Eugene had felt too squeamish for late-night trysts, they'd had plenty of chances. Nearly every evening, Mr. Keliher, who had a third-degree black belt in aikido, went to the *dojo,* and Mrs. Keliher played tennis; the previous Saturday, the Kelihers had been gone the entire day, driving to Yokota Air Force Base to shop at the P.X. and commissary. Yet Nikki chose to shun these gifts of opportunity, dragging Eugene out once again to see the sights: the Tokyo Tower, the Imperial Palace, the Meiji Shrine, the trendy shops and cafés on Omotesando Boulevard, then, at night, the neon jamble of discos in Roppongi and Akasaka, capped off with last call at Flashbacks. Nikki couldn't sit still. "Let's *do* something," she would say. It was as if she were trying to quell his libido with a forced march of tourism.

At the very least, she could have been a better guide. This, Eugene knew, was not the real Tokyo, the real Japan. Nikki had been here only twice before on Christmas vacations, so what she showed him was *Baedeker's* version of the Land of the Rising Sun, a bland, vaguely Asiatic metropolis that was not markedly different from any other big city. Buildings and streets and subways and stores—all homogenized and sanitized and Americanized, with more Kentucky Fried Chickens and McDonald's than he could count.

But Eugene managed to be charmed by the Japanese, by the small courtesies inherent in their everyday interactions. No one appeared to yell in this country except to shout, when you entered and left a store or restaurant, welcome— *"Irasshaimase"*—and thank you—*"Domo arigato gozaima-su."* They apologized profusely for the slightest delay, the tiniest mistake. They bowed, they stammered, they giggled, they avoided confrontation at all costs. Yet they got absolutely goofy-headed about anything different or odd or foreign. Everything was awesome, cute, fantastic. *Wa, sugoi! Kawaii ne! Honto-ni subarashi!* It really was a country like no other. Eugene felt safe and at home here, able to pass for Japanese until he opened his mouth, and more than once he half wished he was Japanese, that he was one of them, one of these gentle, kind people.

▪　　　▪　　　▪

IN the morning, he awoke to the shuffling of slippers and the swishing of kimonos—the maids, whom he seldom actually saw, quietly moving about. He got up and went down the hall to the bathroom, and when he came back to his room, not more than five minutes later, his futon had been put away and replaced with breakfast on the lacquer table. In keeping with the inn's Buddhist monastery theme, there was some dried fish, green tea, rice, pickles, *miso,* and a raw egg.

Nikki and her parents were waiting for him in the courtyard, which featured a carp pond and a water wheel.

"Here he is," Mr. Keliher said. He looked out of scale in the small garden, his head almost level with the eaves of the tiled roof. He was six foot seven, handsome, with blond hair and sideburns and gold-rimmed glasses. He'd been a star forward on the Yale basketball team, a member of Skull & Bones. The four of them stood by the pond, watching the colorful carp. "Did you eat your breakfast?" Mr. Keliher asked Eugene.

"I wasn't really hungry."

Mr. Keliher smirked. "I thought you wanted to experience the real Japan."

"I'd trade tradition right now for a cup of coffee."

Nikki mussed his hair. "Poor baby. You've just been deprived this whole trip, haven't you?" She smiled sweetly at him, doe-eyed with her bangs, then slyly ran her hand down his back to the seat of his jeans and, while her folks were looking away, jabbed her finger at his anus, making him yelp and bump into her mother, who was dragging on a Marlboro.

"Sorry," he said.

Mrs. Keliher blew out smoke—a compressed upward burst from the side of her lipsticked mouth. "Are you all right?" she asked, squinting one eye. Physically she was an older, more stylish version of Nikki, but she seemed—Eugene was quite sure of this—entirely devoid of a sense of humor.

"Sorry," he said again.

Nikki was laughing, enjoying herself. She was like this—utterly unpredictable, distant one moment, affectionate the next. "I'm allowed my contradictions," she had once told him. "It's part of my charm." He had learned to be patient with her moods, which did indeed fascinate him about her. Eventually, she always came around. That was why he wasn't as concerned as he should have been about her recent aloofness, or her imposition of abstinence, or her sudden decision not to go down to Los Angeles with him after graduation, as they had planned, instead enrolling in an intensive Japanese language course at Sophia University and arranging to live with her parents, whom she often said she couldn't stand.

"Okay, let's go, *ikimasho,*" Mr. Keliher said, clapping his hands.

The inn provided bicycles for them, and, single-file, they took a long, leisurely ride to the base of the neighboring mountain. After going to the summit on a gondola, they rode back to the village and had a wonderful lunch of *yakitori*—pieces of chicken on bamboo skewers, cooked over charcoal—washed down with beer and *sake.*

A bit unsteadily, they remounted their bikes and made their way to a fishing cooperative alongside a fast-running stream. There, towering over an attendant who wore waders and coveralls, Mr. Keliher expounded on the finer points of *tenkara,* a traditional Japanese method of fly fishing.

"Keep the fly on the surface of the water for only a second, then recast," he said, demonstrating with his bamboo rod, rhythmically flipping the line back and forth. "Forget everything and just focus. It's a matter of *zanshin.*" He closed his eyes, and somehow managed to touch the fly down three times on the same spot.

"*Wa, subarashi!*" the attendant said.

Mr. Keliher smiled. "*Nan-demo nai desu,*" he said modestly.

It was a neat trick, and Eugene wondered how many times Mr. Keliher had practiced it. For all his Zen homilies, he was a fatuous man, given to self-adoration. He considered himself an expert on all things Japanese, even though he had only lived in the country for a couple of years.

They each grabbed a rod, and Eugene and Nikki wandered downstream. They found a nice spot around the bend, out of sight from her parents.

"It's beautiful here," Eugene said. There were cedar and beech trees around them, and, down below, a field of pink vetch. It was much cooler and drier in the mountains than in the city, and the air smelled clean. He imagined the country-side in Korea looked like this; Seoul was a mere two hours away by plane. "Isn't it beautiful?"

"You're so happy all the time," Nikki said. "Why are you so happy?"

"What's wrong with being happy? I'm happy being with you. You make me happy."

Nikki rubbed her nose and stared at him. "There's some-thing wrong with you," she said. She held up her fishing rod. "Let's try Daddy's technique." She put her hand over her eyes, swung the rod, and the line whipped behind her, the fly with its hook snapping the air three feet from Eugene's head.

"Hey. Careful."

"Hm. Maybe I need more practice."

She took off her sandals and waded into the stream. She was wearing running shorts and a denim shirt, the tails tied around her waist. Her hair—wavy and brown—was loose over her shoulders, and her skin was tan. She was small-framed, with tiny features—little mouth, little nose, on a lit-tle round face with dimpled cheeks—but there was a voluptuous quality about her, earthy and sensual.

"Stay like that," he said. "Let me take a picture of you. You look very sexy like that."

"You think?"

"Yes," he said, pressing the camera's shutter.

Nikki set down the fishing rod, walked over to Eugene, and kissed him, then tugged on the zipper of his jeans.

"What do you think you're doing?" he said.

"I guess I just crumple into submission whenever I hear a compliment."

"We can't do this here."

"We can't?" she said, fondling him. "You don't want to? You're going to re*fuse* me after all that hounding? What are you, a tease?"

"I *want* to, but someone might see us."

"I think it's very evident that you *want* to."

From upstream, he heard the trill of a referee's whistle, as if in admonition, an order to cease and desist immediately. "Just perfect," Eugene said.

"I didn't hear anything."

"C'mon. We have to go." The fishing attendant had explained to them that there was a ritual at the cooperative: when someone caught a fish, he would blow his whistle, and the others should gather for a group photo.

Nikki still had him in her grasp. "Stop squirming. We don't need to go anywhere."

"Your father caught a trout. They'll be looking for us."

"Fuck 'em. Just relax, Eunice." Her pet name for him.

"Let *go* of me, Nikki," he said, and nudged her away. He hadn't meant to be so abrupt, and he could tell she was dismayed with him. While he gathered their fishing poles and her sandals, she stood still, gazing at the field below, and when he held out the shoes to her, she wouldn't take them.

"I know, I know," Eugene said. "I don't have a spontaneous bone in my body."

She slowly lifted the sandals from his hand. "Sometimes," Nikki said, "you make me very sad."

■　　　　　■　　　　　■

BEFORE dusk, while the others napped at the *ryokan,* Eugene ventured out for a walk, and soon found himself lost. When he stopped a farmer for directions, he realized that not only did he not know the inn's address, he did not know the inn's name. *"Sumimasen, doko ryokan?"* he asked stupidly with the few words he possessed. *Excuse me, where inn?*

By the time he stumbled back upon the *ryokan,* he had walked at least seven miles. It was now dark, and he was late for dinner. A maid anxiously ushered him to Mr. and Mrs. Keliher's suite, which was palatial compared to his room, three times the size, with floor-to-ceiling *shoji* screens that opened to the courtyard. Nikki and her parents were sitting on the *tatami* around a table, picking over appetizers, and she and her father wore *yukatas,* long, cotton, kimono-shaped robes supplied by the inn. They had indulged in the *ryokan*'s large communal baths, which were fed by underground thermal springs.

"You've got to try it," Nikki said. "You won't believe how relaxed you'll feel. There's a water slide in the women's bath. Is there a slide in the men's bath, Daddy?"

"No, there isn't."

"Ha!" she said. "You boners."

She was in fine form, and Eugene quickly understood that all three of them were quite looped. There was beer and *sake* and a bottle of Johnny Walker Red on the table, and as the second course was being served, Mr. Keliher ordered another bottle of the Scotch.

The meal came in a flurry—the maids had been waiting for

Eugene—and, in contrast to breakfast, it was a feast. More appetizers and pickles and vegetables, *tempura* and *shabu-shabu,* everything beautifully arranged on small ceramic plates and bowls.

"Eugene, I ordered something special for you," Nikki's father said when the maids returned with yet another course.

It was a fish, a whole fish, with its body sliced and fanned into *sashimi* pieces, its head and tail propped up as if it were still alive, breaching the water.

"What kind of fish is this?"

"It's *koi ikezukuri.*"

"Sorry?"

"*Koi.* Carp."

Eugene turned to the courtyard. "From the pond?" he asked.

"Don't be silly. That would be barbaric," Mr. Keliher said. His wife made a move toward the fish, but he waved her off. "Jo, let Eugene try it first. He's our guest of honor tonight."

This sudden excess of hospitality seemed suspicious to Eugene, and he wasn't a devotee of raw fish to begin with, but nonetheless he grabbed his chopsticks and began to lift off a piece. The fish moved. It seemed, actually, to flinch. "Jesus Christ," he said. It *was* still alive.

Mr. Keliher and Nikki shrieked. "Did you see his face?" Mr. Keliher said, laughing.

"How is this possible?"

"It takes the skill of a master sushi chef—he slices and dices, but he leaves the internal organs intact. Watch this." He poured a cup of *sake* into the fish's mouth, and the fish gulped. Mr. Keliher plucked up a piece of the fish, held it between his teeth for a second, then tipped his head back and slurped it down. "Yummy," he pronounced.

Nikki followed suit. "Yummy," she agreed.

"You look a little pale there, Eugene," Mr. Keliher said.

"Try it," Nikki said.

"I don't think so."

"Don't be such a poop. Live a little."

The hallway screen slid open a crack to reveal a rotund, elderly woman in a resplendent kimono. "*Gomen nasai. Chotto shitsurei shimasu,*" she said in a singsong, bowing, her eyes averted from the room.

"*Ah, konban wa, okami-san,*" Mr. Keliher said. "*Dozo yoroshiku.*"

The woman entered the room, gracefully gliding across the *tatami* on her knees while bowing continuously.

"Our landlady," Mr. Keliher said. He introduced each of them, then offered her a Scotch. She demurred and accepted *sake* instead, and she held the thimble-size cup with both hands and directed it to each of them, bowing, repeatedly cheering "*Kampai,*" before drinking.

Nikki's father then engaged her in a somewhat lengthy conversation, and Eugene gathered from her reactions— politely trying to hide blips of confusion—that either Mr. Keliher's Japanese wasn't as good as he believed or he was drunker than Eugene had thought. Her eyes glazed a little— how many times an evening did she have to greet her guests and listen to them ramble?—but she kept smiling until Mr. Keliher gestured to Eugene, who heard his last name, Kim, being mentioned, along with the word *hero*. The landlady blanched.

Mr. Keliher laughed, and she laughed, too, but clearly she hadn't appreciated the remark, for she left the room soon afterward.

"What did you say to her?" Mrs. Keliher asked.

"Oh, a little joke. I told her Eugene's Korean, and his name's Kim, but I didn't think he was related, and I'd checked and he didn't have any explosives on him."

"What?" Eugene asked. Nikki and her mother were equally baffled.

"I guess she didn't like that," he said. He poured himself another Scotch and explained that in 1968, a Korean man named Hi Ro Kim, armed with a rifle and dynamite, had holed up in a *ryokan* in Sumatakyo, taking the inn's owner and family and several guests hostage for five days. Kim had insisted on daily press conferences, in which he detailed the discrimination he had faced as a Korean living in Japan. The incident had stirred old resentments in both Korea and Japan and had depressed tourism in Sumatakyo for years.

"Brady, you thought that would be funny?" Mrs. Keliher said, vexed. "Are you that sauced?"

"Yes, really, Daddy," Nikki said, giggling.

"All right, *mea culpa.*"

"Honestly," Mrs. Keliher said. "What were you thinking?"

"*Okay*, Jo." He pinched three pieces of the carp between his chopsticks, slathered it in soy sauce, jammed it into his mouth, and chewed it down without joy. "I just find it interesting that our young Mr. Kim here has become such an admirer of the Japanese, considering his people's history. Hasn't your father related his feelings about the Japanese to you?" The Kelihers had met the Kims for dinner at the Fairmont Hotel on graduation night.

"Of course he has," Eugene said. In truth, he knew little about his father's life in Korea before he had immigrated to the States. Out of reticence or bitterness, he wouldn't discuss it. Ironically, because he had been born and raised under Japanese rule, he was fluent in Japanese, and he had ended up teaching it at the Defense Language Institute in Monterey to military officers and spooks like Nikki's father.

"I love this country," Mr. Keliher said, "but the Japanese are the most duplicitous people I've ever known. You can't ever trust them. They never say what they mean, they never mean what they say. They're perfidious. You need to understand that, Eugene. That's all I'm trying to say."

The four of them stared glumly at the half-eaten carp, which still pulsed faintly, and they hardly spoke as the table was cleared and they were given tea and dessert—grapefruit jelly in delicately carved rinds.

"Well, this is cheery," Nikki said.

"I'm sorry, sweetheart. Did I kill the mood? I did, didn't I?"

Nikki nodded. "You've been a real big downer. You ought to be punished. You ought to be *filleted.*"

"Is that right?"

Naughtily, she said, "Tumblelina needs to teach you a lesson."

He brightened. "Oh, it's been years. But do we have enough space in here?"

Nikki smacked the table with both palms. "Tumblelina!" she insisted.

"Okay, muffin. You're on."

They sprung up and moved the table to the side. "Give us some room here, bud," Nikki said to Eugene, kicking him with her toe. She tightened the sash on her *yukata,* then turned around and lunged at her father. He caught her hand and wrist cleanly in midair and pulled her one way and then another and spun her in a half flip until she tumbled onto the *tatami* on her back, slapping her arm down with an earsplitting report.

"Good!" Mr. Keliher said. "You still remember how to roll."

"What the hell?" Eugene said.

"Don't worry," Mrs. Keliher told him. She was sitting against the wall beside Eugene, tamping ashes from her cigarette into her cupped palm. "They've been doing this since she was a kid."

It went on like this, Nikki leaping up and rushing her father, only to be deflected with another aikido move and thrown to the floor, culminating with her hand spanking the straw mats to break the momentum of her fall. She was flushed and breathing hard, and although her father had yet to break a sweat, both of their *yukatas* had come loose, flesh and underwear in plain view.

"Hey, enough," Eugene said, getting up. "That was a very nice demonstration, but—"

Nikki dove at her father, rolled, and slapped.

"Stop it now," Eugene said, and he stepped between them just as Nikki was bulling forward. She knocked Eugene into her father, who locked his arm and whirled him violently in a circle and then flung him to the floor, making him tumble—

couldn't stop—into the *shoji* screen, his foot ripping the rice paper and splintering the lattice.

"Oops," Mr. Keliher said.

"Eunice, you idiot."

From his twisted, upside down position on the floor, Eugene noticed the landlady peeking into the room, hand over mouth, and he wondered what she was thinking then, seeing these *gaijin,* these crazy foreigners—half-naked American father and daughter, standing over defeated Korean lover—disgracing her lovely inn.

   ▪   ▪   ▪

THAT night, with everyone in the *ryokan* asleep, Eugene decided to take a bath. He slipped into the men's *ofuro,* disrobing in the dark, and padded across the marble floor. He eased into the pool of scalding mineral water, breathing in the steam, the sodium chloride, the fragrance of the cypress paneling, and what smelled like cigarette smoke.

"Mrs. Keliher?"

"Hi, Eugene."

Through the steam and darkness, he vaguely made out her head, the ember of her cigarette. She was on the other end of the pool, about twenty feet across from him. "This is the men's side," he said.

"I didn't think anyone else would be here. The men's side is bigger and nicer than the women's—exactly as I'd figured. How's your shoulder?"

"A little sore, but I'll survive."

"Good," Mrs. Keliher said.

They sat there for a while in the heat of the bath, Eugene

beginning to feel loose and light-headed, sweat dripping down his face.

"My husband's a grade-A asshole," Mrs. Keliher said.

"You don't have to apologize for him. No permanent damage done."

"He manipulates people for a living, and Nikki's just like him—spoiled and selfish."

"Well, I wouldn't go that far."

"She's been planning to break up with you, but she hasn't had the guts to do it."

"She told you that?"

"No, but it's pretty obvious, isn't it? What do you call hot-and-cold? Spells *sayonara* to me." When Eugene didn't answer her, she said, "You don't believe me."

"No. I don't."

"Eugene, I'm not trying to play with your head. You're too gullible to see this yourself. When you go back to California tomorrow, you should just forget about Nikki. You'll think it's the end of the world, but it's not. You'll fall in love a dozen more times, and each time you'll think you've learned something, but—you know what?—you won't. You end up with people like Brady because it's practical. It's easier with someone your own kind, you see? Believe me, you'll thank me someday for telling you this."

He didn't believe her, mostly because Nikki came to his room later that night and made love to him and told him that she would miss him terribly, and all summer long she dispatched cutesy letters to him with X's and O's and sexual innuendo, while he worked in a pathology lab, put down a deposit on an apartment for them, and miserably awaited her arrival. At the end of the summer, on the phone, she said she wouldn't be going to U.C.L.A. after all, and then—apology turning into argument—admitted that she couldn't imagine a future with him. She feared he would bore her to death.

■   ■   ■

WHEN he got home from the oncology conference, Eugene helped his wife, Janet, settle their kids into bed, lingering with his eleven-year-old son, Billy, who had a stomachache.

"I might have cancer," Billy said. Recently he'd learned more about what his father did for a living, and now every ailment was a carcinoma. "It might be Stage Four already. I don't know if chemo or radiation will do anything."

"Billy, you don't have cancer."

"I guess we'll have to wait for the lab results," he said, yawning.

Eugene went to the kitchen, where Janet was heating leftovers for a late dinner. While they ate at the kitchen table, he told her about seeing Nikki at the airport.

"I can't believe you didn't talk to her," Janet said.

"What would have been the point?"

"Aren't you curious what's become of her?"

"No."

"Liar."

It had been such a mystery to Eugene—why Nikki had broken up with him, whether race had had anything to do with it, or whether she had simply thought him too dull—but he had stopped dwelling on it long ago. He had a full life, with his children, his wife, his patients. He told himself that Nikki was significant merely because she had been his first love, and that, as cruel as she and her parents had been, they had only wanted to save themselves—and him—some pain.

Janet and her family knew more about hardship than he ever would. She was half and half. Her father had been a black sergeant stationed in Seoul, her mother a Korean national who was disowned over the marriage. The white wives on Yongsan Eighth Army Base had called her a moose, their epithet for any local girl who bagged a G.I. Janet and her siblings grew up in Mississippi, and they had been routinely harassed by their black classmates and called gook monkeys.

Maybe Mr. and Mrs. Keliher had been right: it was easier being with your own kind, you couldn't overcome the hatreds of countries or race, any more than you could forgive someone for breaking your heart.

Eugene had no illusions about how he and his family were viewed in some quarters, but they were happy in Rosarita Bay, which had remained as pastoral and beautiful as he'd remembered it, not unlike that little mountain village in Japan. The people here were civil and polite, and they left their neighbors alone. Out of kindness, they never said what they meant. It didn't matter to Eugene what was really in their hearts, as long as they could live, side by side, in quiet disregard.

YELLOW

AWOMAN from North Carolina—someone he dated for only three weeks in business school—once told Danny Kim that he was lucky not to have the flat nose and dull features characteristic of most Orientals. She had meant it as a compliment of sorts. Her idea of affection was to mock people, and eventually her stereotypes about Asians became a source for her romantic repartee. One morning, after making love throughout the night, she wouldn't let Danny fall asleep, not yet exhausted herself. "You could make me doubt my manhood, pressuring me like this," he said.

"Your manhood," she said slyly, glancing down at his cock. "If I could find it."

But she had loved the way he felt, the sleekness of his body, muscled and long, the face which was at once angular and smooth. What she had said was true, he knew: he was lucky. He had a narrow nose with an adequately pronounced bridge, the epicanthic folds of his eyes were muted, his jaw was square, and he was tall—six-one. He was Asian, to be sure—the straight black hair, raised cheekbones, and olive skin were irrefutable testimony—but the other traits threw people off, no one quite able to get a fix on him. Whites often thought he was Eurasian, some sort of exotic mixture, Malay, French, an Indonesian breed, or perhaps what the Hawaiians called a *hapa,* half-Asian, half-white. Whenever he was introduced to someone, he was invariably asked, "What are you?"—a question he resented more than any other. He never fell into the defensive posturing of some Asians, who would insist, "I'm an American," which would only lead to further displays of ignorance: "No, I mean, what's your *nationality?*"

Yet oddly, it was the Asians themselves, the *sansei* and *yonsei* so sensitive about assimilating, who would most readily ask Danny what he was. Their curiosity had nothing to do with an instilled caste system, the Japanese thinking the Koreans crude, the Koreans believing the Japanese heartless, the Chinese caught somewhere in between. With Danny Kim, they genuinely could not tell, and they could usually tell with astonishing accuracy. Their confusion came as much from the way he carried himself as from his physicality: head up, unhurried in his movements, almost arrogant in the degree of his grace. He always gave the impression, through his faintly cultured manner and cosmopolitan dress, that he was at a remove from whatever was happening around him, and it made people nervous, it seemed he was so self-assured.

And there was that other, incontrovertible factor: he was

handsome. There had been several instances when women, seeing him unclothed for the first time, had told him that he was beautiful, and he remembered being pleased beyond measure then, pleased with the years cultivating each nuance of his personality, with the hours shaping his physique, with how distant he was from the image of himself as a teenager: Dae Hyung Kim, skinny, gangly, his face spotted with acne, unremarkable and unloved in every way.

I.

He was born in 1954 in Rosarita Bay. His parents had immigrated from Seoul just the year before, settling down with the help of some missionaries they'd met during the Korean War. His father, Min Hong, who had been an assistant professor of philosophy at Seoul National University, got a job at city hall as a payroll clerk. His mother, Yong Soo, a petite, elegant woman who, in her time, had been a member of the *jeunesse dorée*—privileged, wealthy, a radio announcer of brief renown in Korea—worked part-time as a florist. They were an incongruous couple, Min Hong taciturn, seemingly passionless, Yong Soo compulsive about appearance, the maintenance of home and family, position. The resident debutante.

Sometimes, frustrated with this new, humbling life, Danny's mother would become shrill, proclaiming she could have married any number of suitors, many of whom were now leaders in the ministry or industrial magnates. Danny's father reacted to these outbursts with utter silence. He was a hardworking man, dedicated to being a good provider, but he had no acumen for business, no ambition to follow the classic rites of other Far Eastern immigrants, beginning with a greengrocery or the like and rising to be an entrepreneur in real estate, owning restaurant chains and factories. And in this country, where his degrees and intellect meant nil, where his English began as passable and would never become quite fluent, he was severely limited in what he could do. Later, he would get a fairly well-paying job teaching at the Defense Language Institute in Monterey, and throughout their children's teens they would be able to gather the accoutrements of the middle class, buying a house, three cars, and the necessary appliances, but Danny would always remember about his parents a forlorn resignation—their youth shadowed by the Japanese annexation, the devastation of two wars, the humiliation of being immigrants.

Of course, then, much attention and expectation were given to Danny. They were, after all, a residually Asian family, and he was their firstborn son. He did not disappoint his parents, at least in any material sense. Predictably, they wanted him to become a doctor or an engineer, and he excelled in the sciences in high school—he had a near photographic memory. But he concentrated, too, on more amorphous subjects. The hours outside school and his job as a stockboy at Safeway, he spent at the movies or in the Rosarita Bay Library. He listened to classical music through earphones, flipped through art books. Mostly, he read novels. He cared nothing for aesthetics or art; his motives were purely utilitarian. He would memorize whole passages from novels and, in private, recite lines with careful enunciation, watching his mouth and tongue in a mirror. His tastes tended toward what he thought was more sophisticated prose—Conrad, Lawrence, Flaubert, Henry James, Fitzgerald—and hence his diction became strangely Anglicized, his expressions formal and stilted. Increasingly, and with unabashed condescension, he would correct his parents' English. Unlike his brother, Eugene, and sister, Lily, he refused to learn any Korean, and when it was used in the house, he would sometimes burst out, "Speak English! Speak English!" His scorn even extended to his mother's cooking: he would not eat any traditional dishes like *pindaettok* or *kimchi,* afraid the sharp smells of red pepper and garlic would linger on him. He rarely brought any of his few friends home with him.

He wanted to be exemplary, unquestionably American. Where this need came from he did not know. There was quite an ethnic mix in the Rosarita Bay school system. The artichoke fields and cannery had brought workers from the cities and migrant families from the San Joaquin Valley to town, and the children of these Mexicans, blacks, Filipinos, and Asians were put together with the Anglos—a practical, rather than necessarily progressive integration—so Danny never had to confront prejudice to any great extent.

Certainly there were incidents, like the time his family had been vacationing in the Sierras and had stopped at a convenience store. A drunk, a big, florid man with his shirt open and his gut out, had staggered up to them. "I forgive you," he had said. "Pearl Harbor. I forgive you for Pearl Harbor." And then he had kissed Danny's father on the *mouth.* Danny had watched horrified. He was appalled by the man, but more so by his father—for letting himself suffer this indignity, then politely *thanking* the man. It had been days before Danny could talk to his father, much less look him in the face.

But that incident alone, or even the accumulation of smaller ones (being called a chink or having people tease him by pulling their eyes slanty), could not wholly account for his vague, perpetual sense of anger. He was, when it came down to it, a proud boy. Although he was an exceptional student and was generally well liked, he did not consider himself popular, and this irked him. He never dated. He felt he didn't have a chance with the fresh-faced, lissome blondes he most admired, and he would not compromise with lesser attractions. Surprisingly, he did not attribute his insecurities to racial difference. Rather, he blamed his acne and the lag in his physical development.

He was always one of the shortest and skinniest in his class, a little kid who needed a bottom-row locker. A saving grace was his natural athleticism. Though he didn't go out for any teams, he accounted well for himself in P.E., especially in swimming and water polo (his mother had nearly drowned as a child, and she had pressed Danny early into swimming and lifesaving instruction through the Red Cross). Then, quite miraculously, the year he was fifteen, he shot up five inches. The rapidity of his growth left him grossly uncoordinated, however, and even skinnier than before. He could hardly run down the field without tripping over himself. With the single-mindedness he applied to everything he did, he vowed, the summer before his junior year, that he would become physically superb.

HE chose to go to the Y.M.C.A. in the Hispanic part of town, a falling-down, decrepit facility where it was unlikely he'd bump into any of his classmates. He would lift weights, he decided, and he half believed his body would be transformed overnight. Yet standing there among the older boys and men as they grunted and strained with their barbells, he felt embarrassed, inconsequential. He would do a few listless repetitions at the bench press, fool with some dips and curls, then leave, his resolve disintegrating with each day. It seemed impossible that he would ever be anything but puny.

Finishing a particularly sluggish workout one night, Danny was thinking he should just quit, give up, when he came out of the weight room and saw a Latino man in the hallway, at the drinking fountain. He noticed him because he was wiry and not very tall, no more than five-five, but was somehow imposing, and neat. Extraordinarily neat. His undershirt and sweatpants appeared to have been ironed. He had a pencil mustache and a pompadour, both meticulously trimmed and looking tidy even now, despite the fact that he had clearly been exercising, a light sweat sheening his skin. His hands were bandaged, and he was washing out a plastic mouthpiece. He took a tiny sip from the fountain, inserted the mouthpiece, and walked down a stairway near the end of the hall.

Danny hadn't known there were any exercise areas in the basement; he had never seen anyone go down there. He followed him. After a wrong turn into the boiler room, he located the man in what he gathered was the boxing room. Danny sat down on a bench near the doorway. The dimensions of the room barely accommodated the boxing ring with its sagging ropes—hugged on three sides by padded walls, laid out flat on the floor, no platform—and the ceiling leaked onto the center of the ring; the man shadowboxed around a trash can which was positioned to collect the drops. There was a speed bag, two heavy bags patched with duct tape, and a wide, full-length mirror, concaved in sections, distorting the reflection. All this was lit by low-hanging fluorescent tubes which made the room too bright; Danny had the impulse to squint as he watched the man.

Danny's only knowledge of boxing before this had been through Muhammad Ali's televised fights—a sport for big men, he had thought. Yet here was this little guy, flashing his bandaged fists, throwing combinations in a blur, bobbing, feinting, moving with remarkable fluidity, a ballet, so light on his shifting feet his shoes did not squeak the vinyl canvas. It was beautiful to watch. It was—Danny knew the word was inappropriate, but he could think of no other—*pretty.*

A bell rang from somewhere. The man stepped out of the ring and toweled his face dry. Running a comb through his hair, he left the room, not glancing at Danny, who was a bit dumbfounded, it had ended so abruptly. He remained on the bench for a while, then finally concluded the workout was finished, the show over, and, disappointed, he walked to the base of the stairs. Then he heard the man coming back down. He quickly returned to his seat on the bench.

This time the man slipped his hands into a pair of boxing gloves. Eyes closed, he stood motionless for a moment, waiting. The bell rang again, and he started hitting the heavy bag, leaning into it with punches. Danny read the label on the bell machine: Ringmaster. He soon understood. The Ringmaster signaled three-minute durations—the length of a round in boxing, he remembered—and the one-minute rest periods in between. The man did three rounds of each exercise, ritualistically toweling, combing, and going to the water fountain between rounds. He never missed a bell, always making it back with a few seconds to spare. On these trips in and out of the room, he wouldn't acknowledge Danny, growing mildly annoyed, perhaps, that he was still there.

After the heavy bag, whanging it with one-two-threes, he moved to the speed bag. The peanut-shaped sack thumped against the platform, rebounding back and forth faster than Danny could follow it, but the man stayed within its rhythm, hitting it precisely with different sides of his fists. Last was the jump rope, varying shuffle steps, heel-to-toe, double-time, arm crosses, the leather rope whistling the air, slapping the floor. When he was done, the man unraveled the bandages from his hands, rolled them up tight, unscrewed the speed bag from the platform, and packed everything into his gear bag. As he walked out, he hopped up to flick off the Ringmaster.

It was the most impressive thing Danny had ever seen. So contradictory: the grace and economy of each motion, the connotation and promise of brutality. He thought it'd be the best of all worlds to have that power, especially if you were small or slight—to know that if it came down to it, you could drop someone; that you were, despite appearances, lethal, dangerous. Perhaps Danny could never be big, but he might be able to possess this power, and he was determined—instantly, implacably—to try.

He found the man in the locker room, a towel wrapped around his waist. Danny couldn't help staring at his stomach muscles, the rows of them. "Excuse me, is there a boxing program here? Classes?"

The man sighed. He took a bottle of dandruff shampoo off the shelf of his locker. Hanging on a pair of wooden hangers was a dark silk suit, pressed and shiny. "It's ugly, you know. Boxing." He turned to Danny and looked him up and down. "Basketball's better for you."

"I don't plan to do it for a living," Danny said.

"No?"

"No. I'm only interested in training, what you were doing, to get into shape. I'm not the least bit interested in actually fighting."

The man grabbed a woman's clear cosmetics bag—shaving cream, a tube of VO5, deodorant, baby powder inside—from his locker. "Monday, Wednesday, Friday, six o'clock," he said. "Bring a mouthpiece, hand wraps, and a cup."

"What do you mean? Are you going to train me?"

The man waved his hand up, defeated. "It's my job," he said as he headed for the showers.

▪   ▪   ▪

LUIS Portillo was the new boxing instructor at the Y. An instructor who preferred not to have any students. This became clear to Danny on Monday when Portillo rushed him through the fundamentals—the three-quarters stance, the jab, and straight right—and then threw him a headguard and a pair of gloves, and motioned to the ring. "Let's go," he said.

"You must be joking."

"Only way to learn."

As Portillo tied Danny's gloves, he told him, "These here? Eighteen ounces. Pads like bath towels. But they make me tell you this: every time you get hit—and you'll get hit, that's boxing—a blood vessel pops in the brain. You got a zillion, no sweat. But you walk into a punch, an accident, brain slams against the skull, you hemorrhage, you die." He turned on the Ringmaster and removed the trash can from the center of the canvas. "Okay, ready?"

Danny noted that Portillo didn't have headgear. His gloves weren't even properly tied, the ends of the laces simply tucked inside with the hands. The bell sounded. Wide-eyed, alert, Danny went into a crouch, and jerked back when Portillo extended his arm.

Portillo smirked. "Touch gloves. Sportsmanship, okay?"

They circled clockwise. Danny tried a few jabs, none of them coming close, Portillo just swatting them aside. Several times, Danny tried to tandem the jab with a right, lunging as Portillo easily slipped away to his left. After thirty seconds, he was winded and spent. It took all he had to hold his arms up. He'd never imagined three minutes could be so infinite. Portillo began throwing jabs at him, and Danny was incredulous. The man was *hitting* him. This must be against the law, he thought, or at least against the Y.M.C.A.'s principles of good conduct; he was being punched and bullied on his first day of instruction.

At the end of the round, he spat out his mouthpiece, Portillo pulled off his gloves, and Danny walked out, not noticing the blood under his nose until he was in the locker room.

If Portillo was surprised to see Danny come back on Wednesday and the succeeding nights, he didn't show it. He went through two more things with Danny—the left hook, the uppercut—then dropped the lessons altogether and just sparred with him. He no longer restricted himself to a single jab or hook at a time, and he even started taunting Danny, puffing out *boo* whenever he tagged him with a punch. Still, Danny kept returning. After two weeks, his stamina improved, and he could last the round without fading. After a month, he could slip Portillo's jab and poke in a couple of his own. After six weeks, they were going three rounds—laying down a towel to catch the leak during the breaks—and Danny was able to sneak in his right once in a while, nearly hitting Portillo flush, throwing him off balance.

"You Korean?" Portillo asked.

"Yes."

"I thought so. Koreans got the killer instinct."

The next session, Portillo began wearing a headguard, and since it was now apparent that Danny was there to stay, he commenced the training in earnest.

▪   ▪   ▪

DANNY went to the Y three nights a week for the next two years. He'd begin his routine with some stretching, check his technique in front of the mirror, then execute Portillo's floor workout, mixed in with some hard sparring. Most of boxing, Portillo stressed, was conditioning, and Danny did his on the intervening mornings before school. Push-ups, pull-ups, sit-ups, leg raises, neck bridges. Portillo forbade weights—they hampered flexibility—and also, rather than long-distance running, he had Danny perform intervals, first jogging a mile, then doing a torturous series of wind sprints, cooling down afterward with another mile jog. On Sundays, Danny was allowed to rest.

In the initial months, he was sore all the time, groaning and wincing whenever he moved, walking bowlegged, his forearms so tight he couldn't make a fist. It *was* an ugly sport. He'd cramp, pull muscles, get bruised. Portillo was careful—no black eyes, not a mark on the face—but periodically he would clip Danny with a hook and his jaw wouldn't close right for weeks. And the smells. Six people (despite Portillo's attempts to discourage initiates, eventually a handful of kids stayed on and joined Danny) shared the same headgear and set of gloves. Danny learned why pros always bopped themselves on the head in the ring: it was a habit from constantly having to adjust a sweaty, ill-fitting headguard while sparring. And even after showering, he could never quite get rid of the stink of glove leather from his hands.

Yet the physical discipline was exhilarating. He enjoyed the feeling of exhaustion after a workout—a warm, cleansed sensation, the blood flowing, his mind absolutely lucid. And, as he had hoped, his body changed. He gained pounds, his appetite ravenous now. He developed sinewy arms, biceps, the muscles on his back, legs, stomach, everywhere, hard and individually defined.

There was a pleasure, too, in the camaraderie with the other young boxers, who couldn't have been more different than Danny. They ranged in age from fourteen to twenty-six, all Hispanic or black. Some were experienced amateurs, a couple semi-professionals with a dozen smokers behind them. One of them, César, a Chicano the same age as Danny, made a living tarring roofs and was already, Danny was amazed to find out, a father of three. Yet he got along with them all. They were a quiet, curiously gentle group. There were no displays of bravado, no loud machismo in evidence, and this was mostly Portillo's doing. Portillo, who claimed he only took the position as the Y instructor because he thought he'd be paid to work out . . . alone; who was a natural teacher, emphasizing safety, character, as much as skill. He prohibited them from sparring with one another, serving as everyone's partner, sometimes going as many as twenty consecutive rounds a night. He didn't let anyone off easy, yet he could be exceedingly polite, apologizing when he hit someone harder than he had intended.

Danny never got to know very much about his trainer. He pieced together that Portillo was from Guatemala, and until an opponent's thumb tore the retina in his right eye, he had had a bright future as a featherweight, but everything else—even what his day job was—remained a mystery. Nonetheless Portillo had a profound influence on all of them, and, for Danny, boxing was almost the least of it. There was his attention to hygiene (he told Danny to wash his face with Noxzema, not soap, for his pimples), his clothes, his entire manner. He appeared untouchable. Style was intrinsic to class, *dignidad*.

Danny found himself imitating him. The key seemed to be a lack of excess, a measured slowness, in everything Portillo did. He looked like he'd never been in a hurry in his life. He embodied absolute stoicism: giving in to emotion made you weak. What he ultimately said to you was this: I don't need you. And that in itself, that sort of self-possession, attracted you to him.

Just by adopting this attitude as his own, an act of will, Danny felt more confident. He had reason to be. He was in terrific shape. At an even six feet, he still weighed no more than a hundred fifty pounds, but he was strong and quick. If he had to, he could probably lay out the biggest football player on the high school team. And the best part for Danny was that *no one knew.* He hadn't told any of his classmates about the boxing, mostly because, when he was still a neophyte, he worried he might be ridiculed or even challenged. It turned out he liked having a life secret from others. He was happy, perfectly satisfied with the way things were going, until one night, Portillo mentioned that all the boys should think about competing in the boxing tournament next spring, the San Vicente County Amateur Championships.

▪   ▪   ▪

THE training intensified. In the ring, Portillo would hold up punching mitts and call out numerical combinations, "One-two-one-three-bob-four-three," and they would hit the mitts with a jab, straight right, jab, and left hook, bob when Portillo swiped at them, and counter with a right cross and another hook. While being yelled to "stick and move," they would weave under a clothesline stretched across the ring and throw uppercuts, slide to the other side, jab, weave again. With careful supervision, Portillo now had them spar one another, matched deliberately—aggressive fighters with counterpunchers, Mutts and Jeffs (tall/short)—to give them a taste of what they could run into.

All the while, Danny tried to come up with an excuse to bow out of the tournament. What he had hid from everyone was that from the very beginning, each time he climbed into the ring to spar, he was terrified. Thus far, he'd been able to ignore his fear, but now, faced with the prospect of going from the insignificant arena of the basement Y to the large civic auditorium in San Vicente, he could think of nothing else. He knew he wasn't afraid of being hit or hurt. With the protective gear, the twenty-six joints in the hand were more in danger of injury than the head. He wasn't afraid of losing, either. No one would know, what did it matter?

It came time to submit the official entry forms to the competition. After distributing the applications, Portillo took Danny aside. He leaned against the wall and scratched at the corner of his eye, almost bashful—this was plainly difficult for him. "For you, I know it's different," he told Danny. "You got college, maybe you'll be a lawyer someday. You got choices. That's why you could never be pro. You knew that coming in. If you'd said different, I'd have said walk. But you surprised me. You stuck with it. You've become a good boxer."

This was news to Danny. Besides a few words of encouragement here and there, like when he stepped into his jab instead of shooflying it, Portillo had never hinted that Danny's skills were anything but pedestrian. "You mean that?"

Portillo wagged his head grudgingly. "You're no Emile Griffith," he scowled, then he eased up and said, "Hey. You're going to do okay in this tournament," and he slapped Danny upside the head so hard it made his ears sing.

It was a rare paternal gesture—unprecedented, really—and

Danny felt trapped. In the end, he could not disappoint Portillo, such was his respect for the man, and he thought he had no other option than to enter the tournament.

■   ■   ■

DANNY would be competing in the novice division as a welterweight, 147 pounds. He was immediately reassured to see that most of the contestants in his weight class were smaller than he. Trying on the brand-new ten-ounce gloves and headguard provided by the tournament, Danny felt light, fast. He had a reach advantage; if he could stay cool through the three two-minute rounds, not get tempted into mixing it up, he had a competitive chance.

He forgot everything in the opening round of his first bout. His opponent, a black kid named Fedler, had no technique at all. He just came out and threw windmill hooks in a bunch. Danny got smacked with one, and, wild with anger and desperation, he stood toe-to-toe with Fedler, winging punches furiously.

Between rounds, Portillo was *laughing*. "Danny, Danny," he said, shaking his head. "Just stick and move. You got this guy. He's gone. He's got nothing left. Lick him with your jab and move. He won't be able to touch you. Stick, stick, side to side, okay?"

It was okay. Doing what Portillo told him, Danny outpointed Fedler. Three days later, he won the decision over his next opponent, and his next after that.

At home, his mother noticed that his cheek was bruised. "You've been *boxing*?" she said.

As far as his family knew, he had been going to the

Y.M.C.A. merely to exercise, and had turned into a workout fanatic.

"Can we come watch?" his brother, Eugene, asked.

"No."

"Why not?" his sister, Lily, said.

"Say something to your son," his mother beseeched his father, who looked at the bruise for a moment, then said, "Boxing's only for poor people. I thought you're not so dumb."

Danny didn't care. He was exuberant. Portillo told him not to get overconfident, he'd had an easy draw, but he, too, was obviously delighted with Danny's performance. He had made it to the semifinals of the championships.

Very early on, Danny had learned that boxing was about compactness—throwing punches within a tiny circle, the shortest distance to the target. In these three fights, though, he learned something else: you also boxed within concentric dimensions of time. He could anticipate a punch, and would slip and roll, counter. In the ring, he was in a circle of time—as well as space—*inside* of the other fighter's, calmly watching a slower pugilistic future. It was an immense feeling. He began to believe that, just possibly, he might win it all.

He fell apart in the semifinals. He knew he would lose in the first ten seconds. His opponent, Raymond Ríos, was taller than Danny by two inches, and had a whip of a jab. Right away Ríos connected with it, two, three times in succession, and then lit into him with a combination. Danny was startled by the solid impact of the punches, considering how fast Ríos was throwing them; it was like having the blunt end

of a log shoved into his face. Occasionally he saw one coming, tried to block or weave, but it was always too late, his
head knocked back and upward. He was clearly outmatched,
and as the round progressed, he began to panic. He couldn't
do anything. He was helpless. He was reduced to covering
up, not fighting at all. The audience jeered. He'd get battered,
grab Ríos's arms or waist, and hold him in a clinch. Several
times the referee cautioned him to box, to stop holding, to
keep his head up. Danny told himself to move, stick and
move, but Ríos cut him off, quicker on his feet. He blindly
reached for the boy's arms and accidentally knocked the top
of his head against Ríos's chin.

"Stop!" the referee yelled. He pointed to Danny and issued
a warning for a head butt, and then he pointed to each of the
judges. A warning was as good as a foul in the amateurs;
there would be a deduction from Danny's score. "Box," the
referee said.

Eternal, the rest of the round. In the interval afterward,
Portillo pulled the elastic on Danny's trunks out to let him
breathe, squirted water into his mouth, and held an ice bag
against his left eye, which was swelling quickly. César, his
Chicano mate from the Y, acting as the second, squeezed a
sponge on the back of his neck and massaged him. Neither
spoke to Danny. He could sense they were embarrassed by
him. The timekeeper blew his whistle, signaling for the
coaches and assistants to vacate the ring. Just before the bell,
Portillo, inserting Danny's mouthpiece, finally looked at him.
"Be a man," he said.

It wasn't there. He wanted to fight, exhibit some *corazón,*
some heart, but it just wasn't there. He understood now the

root of his earlier fear. The truth had been too basic to comprehend. He had been afraid of exactly what was happening. He had been afraid of being afraid.

Ríos started showboating—the Ali shuffle, bugging out his eyes, jutting out his jaw, talking to him. Most of it was unintelligible, garbled by his mouthpiece, but the mocking was intolerable. Danny wrestled him against the ropes.

The referee commanded, "Break! Stop!" He gave Danny another warning for a head butt; another point would be deducted. There were more jeers from the audience. "One more and you're disqualified, mister," the referee told Danny.

Resuming, Ríos popped him with a punch and said, "'Ello." He did it again and again. *'Ello, 'ello.* Danny thought he was saying *hello,* the way Portillo used to rile him by breathing out *boo* when he hit him. Then he heard him distinctly. Ríos was saying *yellow.* "Yellow," Ríos called him, disgusted.

Danny would never be able to figure out if what he did next was a conscious act or not. Certainly he was aware of the referee's last warning—another butt and he'd be disqualified—but it was, he believed, without premeditation, on impulse, that he leapt forward, head first, at Ríos. Perhaps it might have worked, he could have told himself the fight was stopped on a technicality, if Ríos, at that very moment, had not been jockeying backward, creating a gap between them, a short but conspicuous distance in which Danny's lunge, before his head cracked into Ríos's face, could only be construed as intentional, an overt attempt to end the fight prematurely.

The crowd was stupefied. The referee stepped between them and pushed Danny away, raising Ríos's arm as he led him to the corner, to a doctor for treatment of his nose, which was shattered and gushing blood.

The audience booed, tossed beer cups at Danny. He followed Portillo out of the auditorium. *"Pendejo, maricón,"* people shouted. Coward. Faggot.

I I .

At U.C.L.A., Danny acquired a reputation as a cocky kid—a little smug. This initially astonished him, since he felt shy and awkward all the time, too insecure to utter a peep during the first few weeks of classes. But when he thought about it, he concluded it was only natural. That insolent pose of Portillo's—he'd learned it well. He had also grown into a good-looking young man, his skin clear and smooth finally, and he had retained the athletic grace and conditioning of a boxer, though he would never again put on a pair of gloves, never tell anyone that he had boxed at all. Moreover, his classmates believed he was reticent by choice, and, when he deigned to speak, they thought him witty and sardonic. Encouraged, Danny began to mouth off. He was whip-smart, and he soon discovered that he could keep up with the best of them. It was a heady time. 1972. Vietnam. Nixon. The sexual revolution. In this new social milieu, where he had no history, he found his niche. Never mind that he was filled with self-loathing and doubt. If people saw him as arrogant, with a too-cool-for-you façade, and they *admired* him for it, then that was what he would give them.

He endeared himself to the girls in particular because he could get them to talk about anything. One afternoon, as a freshman, he convinced six coeds in Sproul Hall to describe their masturbation habits (he had read Masters and Johnson and *Cosmo* in the Rosarita Bay Library as well). He lost his virginity to one of the girls, Nancy, the next fall.

He was sharing an apartment in Santa Monica by then, and after attending a party together, he and Nancy went back to his room. They drank a bottle of Ruffino and smoked a thin, crumpled joint that Nancy had been hoarding in her purse. They talked for hours. It was four A.M., and Danny was too scared to touch her.

Nancy yawned. "God, I'm tired. You think I could crash out here?"

"Uh, sure," he said.

Not wanting to be presumptuous, he opened the closet to pull out a sleeping bag. Then he saw that Nancy had made room for him on his tiny twin mattress on the floor, squashing herself against the wall. He got under the covers with her. They were both fully clothed. He lay there silently, thinking he should do something, make a move which was assertive but not too obvious.

"Would you mind if I got undressed?" he asked. "I can't sleep with my clothes on."

"Go right ahead," Nancy said magnanimously.

He was now nude, lying beside her rigidly. Minutes passed. He felt her hand shift under the blanket. She grabbed him, caressed. She rolled over, and they kissed frenetically. He took off her peasant blouse and brushed his palms against her breasts, the skin softer than anything he'd ever imagined. Together they unbuttoned her jeans, pushed them down, and then she sank on top of him and bucked up and down with abandon. Within minutes, she writhed, issued out small, convulsive groans, and collapsed on his chest.

While she was recovering, Danny placed her on her back and began exploring her body. He stroked, kissed, rubbed.

"You're driving me crazy," Nancy said.

He slid into her, controlling the pace this time, going languidly.

"Oh God, *um,*" she said.

They made love once more in the morning. She traced her fingers across the ripples on his stomach. For exercise these days he played squash and lifted weights, but he still did his leg raises and sit-ups.

"I love these. So many little muscles," Nancy said.

"The small perfections are what count," he said.

She licked his belly button.

"Nancy."

"Hm?"

"What if I were to tell you that this was my first time?"

She laughed. "Yeah, right, man," she said, the answer he'd hoped for.

He saw her home. It was delightfully uncomplicated. They weren't obligated to each other in any way. He never slept with her again. He was left with pride, for performing well enough to satisfy her, but also with some confusion. He had

not come. In a corner of his mind, he considered this indica-
tive of some deficiency in his technique or, worse, in his
anatomy. Overall, he felt cheated by the experience.

▪   ▪   ▪

DANNY was opposed to the Vietnam War for all the usual reasons, but something else rankled him. Whenever he watched
the evening news and heard reports about the Viet Cong—the
gooks, their devious guerrilla tactics, the tunnels and booby
traps and snipers—Danny would flinch internally. It was, to
him, a blatantly racist war, as were the last two American
wars. The yellow peril. The Japs, the Koreans, now the
Vietnamese—all of them inhuman and atavistic.

Still, despite his apparent solidarity with the students in
Kerchoff Coffeehouse, the smoky, passionate talk about
American imperialism and the bourgeois establishment,
Danny privately thought, for a brief period, about enlisting.
For him, for any Asian, there were deeper questions of
patriotism which could not easily be ignored—a legacy of
the days of internment. He knew, too, albeit secondhand,
about the very real dangers of communism. When the
North Koreans invaded Seoul, had his parents not escaped
to the countryside, they might have been imprisoned or exe-
cuted, along with many of the intellectuals and aristocrats,
or taken away above the thirty-eighth parallel, never to be
seen again.

In his heart, then, he did not believe in the antiwar movement. He kept his cynicism to himself, of course, and
endorsed it all because he recognized it as fashion, much like
the long hair and bohemian dress, but the Vietnam War

marred these otherwise genial years, and heightened his desire to repudiate his Asian-ness.

This self-conscious mind-set had everything to do with his decision as a sophomore to double-major. Studying mechanical engineering, he became all too aware that the campus was separated by a demilitarized zone of its own, the North housing the arts and humanities, the South the sciences, which were dominated by Asians. The stereotypes which traditionally befell science majors were racially endemic at U.C.L.A.: thick glasses, a calculator on the belt, high floodwater trousers. They were, in short, regarded as geeks, goofballs, and Danny thought the Asians themselves were as much to blame as anyone. They were too insular, provincial, and it was true: they were hopelessly square. He defected to the English department. Since math was effortless for him, he continued his engineering courses on the sly, but as far as most people knew, he was exclusively steeped in, say, the Metaphysical poets, Donne's conceit of a compass as close as he got to vectors and wave diffractions.

Actually, as much as Donne's love poems would have been appropriate for them, Danny got to know Jenny Fallows in a seminar called "The Martyr in the Novel." He had been observing her for quite a while—hanging around with drama-student types who wore black and smoked Gauloises. She was exquisite. Heavy, lush hair hanging down her back, milky skin, eyebrows thick and dark. She had a shape to her, too, which made him weak. Wonderful legs. The curve of her breast visible through a loose, sleeveless blouse. Once, they had eyed each other while passing outside of Powell Library.

He noticed that her mouth protruded because of a slightly crooked tooth. He liked it, that single flaw.

Not long into the seminar, they met by chance at the Nuart, the retrospective theater, where *To Catch a Thief* was playing. Inside, he turned and saw Jenny sitting at the end of the same row. She moved to the seat beside him. "This is a coincidence," she said.

Flustered, he looked down at the floor. She was wearing pointy red suede boots. "I like your shoes," he told her.

"Thanks," she laughed, showing her crooked front tooth.

After the movie, they went to a coffee shop, Zucky's. She drank tea and watched him eat. "Do you know about François?" she asked.

"François?"

"I live with him. He's a director. Or he's studying to be one."

"I assumed there was someone. I didn't know his name."

"We can't see each other. Not the way you want. This is special. François just happens to be away."

He tilted his head, bemused—a practiced gesture. "What makes you think I'm interested in you in . . . 'that way'?"

She rolled her eyes, irritated. "Don't be coy."

They went to class together, sometimes lingered afterward for coffee, analyses of *Lord Jim* and *The Great Gatsby*.

She got his address somehow and began sending him things in the mail, odd little clippings. There was a diagram of the constellation Orion, with Jenny's scrawled caption: "Orion has a zipper, a fly. There are subliminals in the sky, you know." A page from her childhood coloring book of a little girl crayoned black: "I've always believed in racial balance." And a photograph of Brando from *Last Tango in Paris*: "He accepts no substitutes. Only real butter will do."

Danny waited. It was only a matter of time. Finally, she told him François would be away again, a film project in the Mojave Desert. Several days of clouds, then a gorgeous afternoon. After class, Danny invited Jenny for a ride in his newly purchased car, a red Porsche coupe. His neighbor, a former race-car mechanic, was leaving for England and had to get rid of it; he practically gave it to him. Danny could not believe his luck. The body was badly dinged up and rusted, but the engine, as expected, was precisely tuned, and whatever its condition, it was a *Porsche*. He loved the car—opening it up on I-5; downshifting into a corner and accelerating out of it; plunging down the narrow entrance to his apartment building's underground garage, gliding into his slot with the engine purring.

"Do you like it?" he asked Jenny.

"What is it with men and their cars?"

He took her up Topanga Canyon, to a spot with a high view of the ocean. He had a cooler in the trunk with cold fried chicken and beer, the lunch Grace Kelly and Cary Grant had shared in *To Catch a Thief*. Every other night for a week, Danny had thrown out the old chicken, fried a fresh batch.

They made love that day. They cuddled on his bed, and she said that as a child, she had pronounced "bedraggled" as "bed-raggled," because that was what her parents looked like on Sunday mornings.

"I think I'm going to be bed-raggled with you a lot," she said.

He knew then that he would fall in love with her.

■   ■   ■

FRANÇOIS proved difficult at first (tears, begging, then recriminations), but eventually, after about a month, he found his own place. Danny was relieved. He had hated the forced civility with François whenever he picked Jenny up, had driven himself sick thinking they still slept together. Exasperated with the delay, he had asked Jenny to move in with him. "I can't," she had said. "I need my independence. I can't just rely on men, jump from one to another. You understand, don't you?"

When François finally did leave, she took on one room-mate, then a second, to split the rent on the one-bedroom apartment—two lonely girls who stayed home all the time in a nihilistic funk. Jenny spent nearly every night at Danny's.

They were consumed. They saw no one, lost touch with all their friends. Frequently on weekends they did not leave his room. Sometimes they forgot to eat.

By then Danny thought of himself as relatively experienced. He had had a healthy string of affairs, and though often he was still too mindful of his performance to enjoy the sex, he no longer questioned whether he was adequate, anatomically or otherwise. Yet once he began sleeping with Jenny, he discovered just how much he didn't know—all the subtle ministrations which could only be learned through daily intimacy. She taught him everything.

Their bodies fit together perfectly, a natural confluence.

They had their routines, their preferences. At night, slow kisses, brushing of lips, Danny sliding down. Then he'd rise above her, be inside, hold himself up to watch her face, pressing against her while he moved at once circularly and contrapuntally. She would touch his nipples, run her nails lightly down the hollow of his back, between his buttocks. When one sensed the other getting close, it'd push them both over. Without miss, the first time, every time, they came simultaneously, a fact of which they were ridiculously proud.

In the morning he'd wake up with Jenny spooned in his lap. There was so much made of the male genitalia, he thought, but women . . . they had their differences, too. He'd curl against her, his morning erection spreading her distended labia—unusually exposed, a protrusion not unlike her mouth's—and he could not wish for anything sweeter, not entering yet, just rubbing along the furrow of this warm, plummy flesh.

During the summer, Danny worked at a firm which designed oil drilling equipment, Jenny at a nursery. These were idyllic days. Drives on Pacific Coast Highway, gin and tonics, walks on the beach, reading passages from *A Sport and a Pastime* to each other, slow-dancing to Dinah Washington, cooking elaborate meals.

Danny was delirious. He was in love, wildly happy, and, as a consequence, he was sadder than he'd ever been in his life. He despaired that it couldn't last, it had to end. Irrational as it was, he suddenly believed that Jenny would break his heart. Sometimes he'd accuse her of being unfaithful to him, of having fallen in love with someone else. She was capable of it once, why not again? "Why are you doing this?" she'd cry.

In July, they thought she was pregnant. She wasn't, but

before they were sure, he asked her to marry him.

"Oh, sweetheart, it'd be foolish," she said. "You'd always blame me for trapping you."

"No, I wouldn't."

"Yes, you would. In the back of your mind, you would."

"But I love you. I want to marry you."

"I know. But the timing's all wrong. We have to finish school first and decide what we're going to do with our lives." She told him she would get an abortion.

"Would you feel all right about doing that?" he asked her.

"Yes. Because I can't imagine that we won't have children together someday, that we won't get married."

They drove up into the Hollywood Hills that night. The Santa Ana winds were blowing, desert air buffeting the trees, and with the smog cleared out, they had a spectacular view of the city lights. "What do you think our kids would look like?" she asked.

It took him a moment to understand; somehow he had never thought of race as an issue, a complication, with Jenny. "They'd have straight, brownish hair and brown eyes," he said. "They'd either be beautiful or homely. With mixed-blooded children, there are no in-betweens."

Jenny kissed him. "We'll have three. Two boys and a girl. They'll all be beautiful."

He should have been appeased. Instead, he was convinced more than ever that the romance was blighted.

▪   ▪   ▪

THEIR senior year began. Danny was often moody. Whenever Jenny tried to nudge him out of it, he'd become more distant from her. Their studying sessions—before, filled with sighs, wistful looks—were now dry, businesslike. They no longer made love every day.

One afternoon, as they were walking on campus, they passed a group of male Asian students. One of them, under his breath, said, "Banana."

"What did he mean?" Jenny asked Danny when they were out of earshot.

He was tight-lipped.

"What?" she asked again.

"Yellow on the outside, white on the inside," he told her.

"That's hilarious! Banana! Now, is 'Oreo' the same kind of thing? I thought it meant—how can we put this delicately—a double-entry transaction."

"I don't know."

"Food epithets . . . there must be something significant about that, don't you think?"

Sullen, he would not respond.

She flew to Minneapolis for Thanksgiving vacation. He would join her and meet her family for the first time. The night before he was to go, he saw a classmate, Paul, his squash partner. They went to a bar they used to frequent, a noisy place known for their cheap drinks. It was mostly a college crowd, and Paul was looking at the girls. A pair in particular, across the dance floor, intrigued him.

"The blonde?" Danny asked.

"More your speed, not mine," Paul said. "The Nebraska farm girl who's come to the big city and become sophisticated and signed up with the intelligentsia but who retains her inherent wheat-field glow."

"Is that how my tastes come off?"

"It's shameful how predictable you are."

Paul liked the other girl—tiny, with wavy brown hair—and he enlisted Danny to approach them. While Paul danced with the brunette, Danny was left with the blonde. Small talk. He had no intention of going beyond mere conversation, regardless of how tenuous things were with Jenny, but he couldn't help trying to win her over, anyway. He was not immune, in these situations, to needing his attractiveness reaffirmed.

The blonde was uncooperative. She was polite, answering his questions, but her attention drifted. "Listen," she said eventually, "you shouldn't waste your time on me."

"Pardon?"

"You're very nice, really good-looking. There are plenty of girls here who'd love to go out with you."

"But not you."

She shrugged.

"Why not?"

"It's nothing personal," she said.

"What is it, then?"

"It just wouldn't work out. Can't we leave it at that?"

"No," Danny said, feeling contentious. "I want to know."

"Okay," she said uneasily. "I'm sorry. I don't date non-whites. I just wouldn't be able to handle it."

He was so vain, it had never occurred to him that he would have no chance at all with a woman, that he could be summarily dismissed, simply because of the color of his skin.

▪   ▪   ▪

MR. Fallows was an executive with Northwest Airlines; Mrs. Fallows, a former flight attendant, ran her own travel agency. Their house was in Edina, an affluent Minneapolis suburb, filled for Thanksgiving with Jenny's many siblings and relatives. Danny felt overwhelmed, and his discomfort swelled when he was introduced to the grandmother. She was clearly confused. "Are you from Vietnam?" she asked.

She had been hearing about the recent wave of Vietnamese, Laotian, and Cambodian refugees, and was stuck on the idea. Even after his clarification, she continued to think Danny was an F.O.B.—Fresh Off the Boat. "How do you like the United States?" she asked.

Jenny giggled. "Grammy, he's lived in California all his life."

After grace, everyone raised their wineglasses. "Happy Thanksgiving," they said to one another. The grandmother warmly saluted Danny: "Welcome to America." Jenny guffawed. She nearly fell out of her chair. It angered him that she found this funny.

The following day she took him on a tour of Minneapolis and presented him to her friends. Later, Jenny told him, "You know what Amy said? She said, 'How come you've come back from L.A. with all these Oriental things? Your purse, your address book, your boyfriend . . .' "

"What did you tell her?"

"That I appreciate beauty. Even Dad says you're—his words—'exceedingly handsome.' He's never commented on any man's looks before."

"What do they think of me? Your family."

"They think you're charming."

"Nothing else?" Danny asked.

"Most people would take that as a favorable ruling, honey."

"They didn't mention anything about my being . . . an Oriental *thing*?"

"Grammy told me you don't *look* that malnourished after all those months at sea."

"No, really."

Jenny smiled impishly. "Kate wants to go to bed with you," she said, referring to her sixteen-year-old sister. "She can't believe anyone's skin can be so tight."

The trip, seeing the cozy, genteel world she came from, made him mistrustful. Her family and friends had been amiable enough, but they didn't seem to attend to him earnestly, as if he were only Jenny's latest distraction, a Japanophile phase she was going through, not as though he were a prospective husband for her. And to Danny, this had to reflect Jenny's own attitude about him.

They took their final exams, and then she left for Montserrat to spend Christmas with her family. Danny went to Rosarita Bay for a week. His relationship with his own family was, at best, perfunctory these days. He had never cared for Jenny to meet them, but during this holiday, he thought it odd that she had not once suggested it herself.

He got home at dinnertime, his parents, Eugene, and Lily already at the kitchen table. They were chomping on *kalbi* ribs, slurping *mandu*. It never ceased to amaze Danny, the noise with which they ate.

"Man, oh, man," Eugene said. With his chopsticks, he wrapped a leaf of lettuce around some *kimchi* and a clump of rice and stuffed it into his mouth. "I've been missing this."

"You're here all the time," Danny said. Eugene, who was a sophomore at Stanford, less than an hour away, was a much more dutiful son than he was, visiting almost every other week.

"*Chal mogo,*" his little sister said. Eat well. Lily, still in junior high school, had recently become a born-again Korean.

"You want more milk?" his mother asked. She was beaming, happy to have all her children at home.

"I'll get it," Eugene said. He stood and opened the refrigerator, banging the door against Danny's chair.

"Hey, watch it."

"Sorry, Danno."

"Why is it that we have a perfectly good dining table in the dining room, and we always eat in the kitchen?" Danny said. "Can someone explain that to me?"

"It's for guests," his mother said.

"What guests? Do you ever have guests?"

"We had a guest for Thanksgiving," Lily said.

"Who?"

"Eugene's new girlfriend. He's in *luuuv.*"

"Is that right?"

Eugene grinned goofily. "Her name's Nikki."

"Are you going to marry her?" Lily asked.

"Maybe. Maybe I will."

"Don't get too carried away," Danny said to Eugene. "You haven't even met her."

"You think it's love, but it's probably infatuation."

"Man, when'd you become so cynical?"

"Trust me," Danny said.

His father, typically nonconversant, not giving them a glance, dipped a stick of cucumber into chili sauce and munched.

▪   ▪   ▪

THEY reunited in L.A. on New Year's Eve. Jenny was tan, gorgeous. "God, I missed you," she said.

A movie producer was throwing a party in his Brentwood mansion. It was a huge affair, at least seven hundred people. Jenny had been looking forward to it all month. She bought a short, red faille dress with a revealing décolletage for the occasion. Danny never fully understood the vague connections—a friend of friends of Jenny's—which put them on the guest list. They knew no one there, but Jenny blithely mingled.

As Danny was following Jenny through a throng in the main ballroom, he noticed two men ahead staring at her, at her breasts, then coolly at him. He and Jenny had to squeeze past them, turn face-to-face with one man to get by. "Did you know it's National Hate Chinese Week?" the man said to Danny.

"Ignore him," Jenny said, tugging him away.

Jenny found some acquaintances to talk to. Danny was standing apart from the group when something hit him on the chest. He looked down at the floor. It was a wedge of lime.

"What's the matter?" Jenny asked, moving over to him.

Another wedge bounced off his temple. Across the room, the two men glared at Danny, sipping their margaritas.

"Come on, let's go out to the lawn," Jenny said.

Sweat trickled down his back. After a moment, he complied.

They didn't stay long. Danny was silent as they drove away from the mansion. He felt murderous. He hated himself for having done nothing. He hated Jenny for dressing like a whore.

"Sweetheart, just try to forget it," she said.

"I can't forget it. It's what I have to live with every day."

"They were just a couple of drunk assholes."

"You have no idea. . . . It's a novelty to you. An interracial couple. So radical-chic. Even more rebellious than shacking up with François. What will it be next? A black guy?"

"That's not fair," she said to him. "Your color's never been an issue with me. I've never even thought about it."

He scoffed.

"It doesn't matter to me what other people think," Jenny said. "I don't care."

"You are laughably naïve."

"Danny, please . . ." She touched his arm.

He jerked away. "Don't," he said in revulsion.

He did not see her for several days. More than anything, he marveled at how deluded he had been, for he had believed—abstractly, quixotically—that he *could* be white. Colorless. He realized he was doomed. No matter what he did, no matter how much he tried to deny it, he would never get past his ethnicity. It was untenable, and the knowledge broke him.

He told Jenny it was over.

"You can't do this," she said.

They argued for many hours, at the end of which he told her, as a coda, "You were never serious about me, anyway."

Sobbing, she slapped him. "I loved you. I wanted to marry you. Don't ever lie to yourself that I didn't."

Danny was speeding as he entered the underground garage of his apartment building. He had wanted to race toward the far wall, stomp on the brakes, skid to a stop an inch away from impact. Someone had hosed down the concrete to clean the garage. The tires locked and slid over the sheet of water, the car's front end crumpled into the wall, and Danny remembered the seat belt roping around his waist as he folded over, his face snapping into the steering wheel.

▪   ▪   ▪

THE surgeries on his nose and cheekbones were reconstructive. The operation on his eyelids was elective, cosmetic. His appearance wasn't altered that much—a little more exotic, more sculpted. He could have returned to school in the spring, but he chose to wait until the summer, until after Jenny had graduated.

He stayed in L.A. for another two years, working as an engineer at Lockheed. For a while, she would call. They had lunch a few times. She looked different, too. Her hair was shorter, and she had braces. She was a production assistant for a film company. Eventually they lost touch altogether.

III.

Danny—or Daniel, as he called himself now—liked the case method at Harvard Business School, and, by and large, he was impressed by his sectionmates. Some were from old money, Brahmins who'd followed the patrician line from St. Paul's and Andover to Harvard and Yale to Goldman Sachs and Morgan Stanley. Danny knew exactly what to expect from them. But the others, especially the midwesterners—they confused him. It maddened him that they were so damn *nice.* He could not accept that there wasn't something specious in these people, these consummately all-American, hardworking, white-bread, smiley-faced dorks. They were just too sincere to be true.

He kept to himself. He rented a studio apartment in the Back Bay instead of living in the B-School residence halls, and while he worked in small study groups, as was dictated by the program, he did not socialize with his sectionmates.

Romantically, too, he was passive. When he was the object of pursuit, he would sometimes try to go through the motions, but he never had his heart in it, and women found his disaffection cruel. "There's something wrong with you," one of them, the woman from North Carolina, said when they broke up. "You're so cold-blooded. You don't have any loyalties to anybody or anything. You know what I think? I think you're incapable of love. I think you're secretly a misogynist."

Eight months later, he married a Korean American. His mother arranged it for him. For years, she had prodded Danny, urging him to go out with a dozen Asian girls, showing him photographs even, and he had refused unequivocally. She had been shocked when he asked her to introduce him to someone.

Rachel Chung, born in Rochester, was the daughter of his mother's schoolmate from Seoul. A senior at Boston University when he met her, she was short but trim, cute with her thick, pageboy hair and rounded mouth. She was companionable, and had her cultural finishes—a theater major who had wandered into costume design—and her values were patently Western, as far removed from the old country as he was.

The night he proposed, she took him back to her apartment. Heretofore, he'd only kissed her. "You don't have to be such a gentleman all the time," she said. They made love. She was the first Asian woman he'd ever touched.

■   ■   ■

FOR five years, he worked at RaycoTech, a semiconductor company in Woburn, outside of Boston on Route 128. Despite the commute, Danny wanted to stay in the city, and he and Rachel bought a condo on Dartmouth Street. He was comfortable in the Back Bay. The neighborhood had a continental atmosphere. The French consulate was just three blocks away, most of the residents were young professionals, and the shops and restaurants were tony, civilized. He felt relatively secure there, whereas elsewhere in Boston and its suburbs, he did not.

He constantly sensed the underpinnings of racial animus in the city, which was so plainly and historically stratified by class and color. At the better restaurants and hotels, at upscale functions and parties, at business meetings, it would dawn on him that everyone there, *everyone*, except him, was white. He felt a kinship with prosperous blacks, a silent brotherhood of tokenism, and was ashamed of himself when he tolerated his colleagues' racist jokes and comments. He shouldn't have been surprised, but he always was, to hear ostensibly liberal, educated northerners using the word *nigger*.

He was more concerned, though, with the hostility toward Asians—specifically the Indochinese immigrants—that he saw increasing with their presence in Boston; he thought he was becoming a victim of it. Sometimes it was subtle. His flight was delayed at Logan once, and he went to the airport bar for a cup of coffee. There was a group of salespeople at the next table, and one of them, repacking her briefcase, pulled out a cellular phone. A man in the group said, "Hey, let me use that portable phone there. I want to call Hong Kong. Order me some chop suey." They laughed. Danny looked over to them, nervously wondering if the joke had been casual or if he was being baited; he felt utterly humiliated. Other times, it was clearer. He was waiting at a stoplight one day, and a man in the passenger seat of the car next to Danny's said, "Fucking Orientals everywhere."

Occasionally, he would tell Rachel about these incidents, and she would tell him about things that had happened to her. She had given up her dreams of an acting career when a famous director, whom she'd approached for advice, had said, "To be frank, honey, there aren't a whole lot of plays with kimonos and rice paddies." But Rachel had more equanimity than Danny. "You have to rise above it," she'd shrug. She didn't like dwelling on the subject, and she would discuss it with him less and less. She was comfortable being Korean, was fluent in the language, and often spoke Korean to both their families in public, which Danny's mother and father loved, while Danny anxiously glanced about them, not understanding what they were saying, sweating.

As the years went by, he grew more alarmed. Racial tensions were peaking. It wasn't just in Boston, either. A jingoistic, reactionary mood was consuming the entire country, and it scared Danny to death. He followed reports on the resurgence of the K.K.K. and white supremacy groups, racial assaults, boycotts of Korean merchants, and, in particular, during the early eighties, events in Michigan, where people threw rocks at Japanese cars, where they organized rallies to sledgehammer Toyotas, where two laid-off auto workers killed Vincent Chin, a Chinese American, smashed his head in with a baseball bat, saying, "It's because of little Jap motherfuckers like you the car industry's going down the tubes," and then got off on probation, never to spend a day in jail.

With all of this happening, then, with the heightening focus on the trade deficit, how could Danny not bristle or feel threatened whenever he was asked "What are you?" or "Where are you from?" He could excuse the question as benign curiosity to a certain extent (those somewhat exotic features), but when he was asked it immediately by absolute strangers, it exposed a fundamental misconception. He was born here, he spoke perfect English, he was as mainstream as anyone could be. Yet, in this country of immigrants, Danny, as an Asian, was always regarded as a foreigner, a newcomer, someone who was not a *real* American. The question, by implication, had less to do with what he was, since precise geographical origins were irrelevant (a chink was a dink was a Jap was a gook), than with what he wasn't. It was a bad time to be Asian in America. Every day he expected, at any moment, at any place, to be attacked.

RACHEL gave birth to a son, Michael Jay Kim. He was a big baby, weighing in at nine pounds. He would be tall probably, but Danny was disappointed with his looks. His head was squarish, his face broad and flat; his black hair poked out as stiff as porcupine quills, and his eyes were cut thin in slits. It was a dull physiognomy, characteristic of Orientals.

"With the amount of time you're home," Rachel's older sister, who was visiting from New York, told him, "it must have been an immaculate conception."

"Beth, don't be *ongtoree*," Rachel said—Korean for *stupid*. "Haven't you ever heard of phone sex?"

"Daniel, Daniel, what do you get when you cross a rooster with a telephone pole?" Beth asked.

"A cock that wants to reach out and touch someone!" the sisters screamed at the same time. They howled, hit each other with sofa pillows.

Danny was unimpressed.

"You're such a poop," Beth said to him. "Don't you ever loosen up, do something besides work? You ever have any fun? Do you *know* how to have fun?"

Later, as they were readying for bed, Rachel asked Danny, "Tell me the truth, are you having any fun? You're so . . . serious all the time."

"I take what I do seriously. Is that a fault?" He arranged

what he would wear to the office tomorrow on his wooden valet: Louis, Boston suit, Hathaway shirt, Charvet tie, cap-toed Brooks Brothers oxfords. Clothes were his one extravagance.

Rachel came up from behind and hugged him. "Sometimes I wish you hadn't taken this job."

RaycoTech had ridden out the computer-industry recession in 1984, but he knew the semiconductor market would remain in a downturn. He got out while he could. In 1985, he joined Delaney, Rhodes & Company, a management consulting firm in downtown Boston.

The hours were grueling, the consultants often called upon at a moment's notice to go to Chicago, Austin, Atlanta, for months at a time. D.R.C. gave them a round-trip plane ticket every weekend, but the strains on family life were inescapably taxing. Even when Danny stayed at the State Street office in Boston, he worked most weekends, and most nights during the week, he came home long after Michael was asleep, too tired to do anything but share a late dinner with Rachel before heading to bed.

Nonetheless, he assumed Rachel was content. He knew she wasn't happy about his workload, and their marriage didn't have a lot of passion, but he thought it was better than most. They had a comfortable life, money, a child, and they talked of having a daughter someday. When Rachel wanted to go back to work as a costume designer for the Huntington Theatre, he encouraged her. After all, Michael had turned five and was attending school now, and Danny could understand if she was a little restless. Then she told him that before a play began its run, she would have to be at the theater at night—

weekends, too. Since daycare ended at six o'clock, he would have to be home by that time during those months.

He didn't know what to say at first, the request was so unreasonable. "What happens if I get an assignment out-of-state?" he said.

"You'll have to give it to someone else."

He had to laugh. "Come on, that's insane."

"Why?"

"I'd be fired."

"No, you wouldn't," Rachel said. "You're too valuable to them. If you really wanted to work normal hours, demanded it, you could. They'd accommodate you."

"Certainly I'll make partner that way. Is this a ploy to get me to spend more time with you and Michael? Because if it is, trying to undermine my career isn't going to accomplish anything."

"What about my career? It's just as important as yours."

"Your sister put you up to this, didn't she?"

"Beth has nothing to do with this. It's us. I don't even know why we're together anymore. Why did you marry me? You don't want to be with me much, that's for sure. Sometimes I think you hate me."

"How can you say that? I don't hate you."

"No, you're right. It's worse. You don't care enough to hate me."

They hired an *au pair* as a compromise, but things were different, they never reached a full level of rapprochement from that point on. He and Rachel were civil to each other, did not complain about a thing, and the underlying resentment was nearly unbearable. Their marriage began to function on the principle of quid pro quo: she played the good wife, he played the supportive husband, and whenever one agreed to go to a party, socialize with the other's friends or colleagues, there was the sense that now there was something *owed*.

He despised her theater friends. They were pretentious, loud, wore too much makeup and clothes much too hip for their age. It wasn't until one Sunday at the movies, though, that he understood his aversion toward them had a secondary, subliminal basis. He went without Rachel or Michael, as was often the case these days, buying a ticket without knowing what the film was about—anything to get out of the house and the summer heat—and as he sat in the air-conditioned darkness, reading the opening title credits, he was startled to recognize a name: Produced by Jennifer Fallows. He had never put the two together, Rachel and Jenny, the latter's clique of drama students at U.C.L.A., François the director, Hollywood.

Over the next couple of weeks, memories visited him, eidetic glimpses of Jenny in the bathroom, wearing his shirt, the tails lifting to reveal her splendid behind as she blow-dried her hair; of her in class, fondling him under the seminar table as she listened, quite primly, to the professor's lecture, which linked *Sons and Lovers* to Freud's Madonna/whore complex; of her dropping a rolled-up note in a bottle of wine they'd just finished, a note he tried to extract with a pencil, a wire hanger, finally smashing the bottle with a hammer to read, the ink running over the wine-bled paper, "I cherish you, I adore you, I love you."

When they had stopped seeing each other, Danny had

promised himself that he'd never risk being so vulnerable again. He had surrendered to the fact that being with an Asian woman was easier, safer. Maybe he hadn't been in love with Rachel in the beginning, but marriage was not built on infatuation, and he would come to be fond of her, he had believed. But along the way, he had sacrificed more than he'd known. He had forfeited that part of himself which permitted the possibility of love.

▪   ▪   ▪

In 1991, D.R.C.'s biggest client was Beal Microsystems, a minicomputer manufacturer in San Jose. It was a huge, intricate job, and Danny was heading D.R.C.'s team with another executive consultant named Kevin Sheridan, an interesting and not entirely coincidental arrangement, since it was no secret that they were competing for a partnership. Danny disliked Sheridan with a passion. They had been assigned together on several other jobs, and each time, Sheridan was industrious only in the variety of ways he invented to avoid or delegate his work. Quite simply—at least to Danny—he lacked the technical know-how to get down to business. Danny wondered how he had squeaked through M.I.T. with an engineering degree, through Boston College with his M.B.A., and he was dumbstruck that Sheridan's deficiencies hadn't caught up to him yet, that he was allowed to stay— indeed, *thrive*—in the firm.

He had to grant him this, though: Sheridan was affable. Taller than Danny, slim, with lank blond hair and an asymmetric grin, he was the personification of old-boy blue-blood charm and assurance (his father had been an economic advisor to J.F.K.). The clients loved him, and he was deft in manipulating that bias. For instance, he was careful in meetings and presentations to give credit where credit was due, but he was always a bit too self-deprecating about his own contributions to the project, leaving the impression that he was being modest. The end result was that when a problem or question arose, the clients asked for *him,* not Danny. It wasn't too difficult to imagine what got back to Dennis Rhodes, D.R.C.'s senior partner.

At Beal Microsystems, there was something even more devious about Sheridan's schemes. They were meeting one day with the operations president, Marc Ballinger, who would make the principal evaluation of their performance to Dennis. Ballinger looked at the results of their computer model, and the news was not good. Even with severe cost-cutting measures and layoffs, Beal would barely be competitive with a Japanese upstart called Teko, which was gobbling up Beal's market share. Uncharacteristically profane, Ballinger muttered, "Fucking Teko. Goddamn Japanese."

For the remaining months of the job, Sheridan tried to engage Ballinger every chance he got in some lusty sessions of Jap-bashing, given to coy little remarks like "Well, we're all white here" and "Ah so" and "Chop chop chop," and launching into diatribes about the trade deficit and Japanese real-estate investments in the U.S., *the buying of America's soul.* "Really, what it amounts to," he told Ballinger, "is economic imperialism."

Harder to read was Ballinger's attitude toward all of this. Other than in that initial meeting, he did not make any more xenophobic comments. Surely he was smart enough to separate Danny, a Korean American who had grown up fifty miles west of Beal's corporate headquarters, from the image of any Japanese rival, but who knew what his personal, visceral feelings were, if he would be susceptible to the subconscious associations Sheridan was trying to instill? Who knew about anyone, for that matter? Danny remembered being shocked when he had heard Dennis, whom he'd admired and trusted more than anyone else at D.R.C., once referring to a client and saying, "It might be messy. He's real . . . Jewish."

Danny tried to talk to Rachel about what was happening. "You're overreacting," she said. "I'm not crazy about Kevin, either, but no one could be that calculating." It was rare for him to seek Rachel's counsel on anything these days, and her quick dismissal of the situation wounded him.

He was convinced that he would not be made partner. A traditional Boston firm like D.R.C. might patronize him, exploit his talents, but it would never grant him full admission.

He and Sheridan wrapped the Beal job a week before Christmas, and, much to Danny's discomfort, they ended up on the red-eye to Boston together. They didn't say much. They exchanged a few final notations and fell asleep. Both were aware that everything was out of their hands now. Most likely Dennis and the other partners had already made their decision. They'd attend D.R.C.'s Christmas party, Danny would go to St. John for a week's vacation, then they'd learn who had been chosen for partner in mid-January.

An hour and a half away from Boston, Danny was awakened for the breakfast service. Groggily he peeled off the foil covering his omelette and tore open the cellophane packet of utensils. He looked to Sheridan, who was in the adjoining

seat. He was staring out the window, and his face was averted, but he was, unmistakably, crying.

"Celie's leaving me," Sheridan quietly said. "Did you
know that?"

"No."

"Of course not. You don't know a single thing about me.
Tell me, how many kids do I have?"

Danny admitted he had no idea.

"Six. I've got six. They're what I live for. And now Celie
wants me to move out. She can't even wait until after
Christmas." He turned to Danny. "Do you love your family?"

Before Danny could answer, Sheridan said, his tone vacil-
lating from maudlin to bitter, "The work we do, it's pointless.
We work like dogs, we kill ourselves nights and weekends,
and when it's all over, what are we going to have? Are we
going to look back and feel we accomplished anything, created anything? We tell companies how to be more efficient,
and a lot of times that means eliminating people's jobs so the
profit margin goes up a few measly points. What is it that we
contribute? The only thing that makes it tolerable"—he
began weeping—"the only thing that makes it worthwhile, is
having a wife and family to come home to. That's it. What
will I do when I lose that?" He closed his eyes and whim-
pered, choking out loud sobs.

At first Danny thought this was some sort of bizarre
trick—Sheridan, in an insipid reversal of tactics, attempting
to illicit sympathy and pass himself off as a conscientious,
God-fearing family man. But then, as he continued to cry,
oblivious to the flight attendants and passengers glancing at

him, Danny became embarrassed for Sheridan. He was repelled by this open display of weakness.

"Get a hold of yourself," he told Sheridan. "Be a man."

They landed, and Danny hurried off the plane, not waiting for Sheridan. He had to get his luggage, though, and Sheridan caught up to him at the carousel. He was composed now, and he stood by Danny silently for a minute or two before speaking. "I never liked you," he said. "I knew guys like you at M.I.T. You get into schools and get these great job offers and promotions because you're minorities, but you won't help anyone except yourselves, you'll only go out of your way for your own kind. I'm not gifted like you. I have to scramble just to be average, and you've never lifted a finger for me because you enjoy it, don't you? You enjoy seeing me fail. You're ruthless."

DANNY accompanied Rachel to a benefit dinner for the Huntington Theatre at the Copley Plaza Hotel. The incident with Sheridan still stung him. He was glad Sheridan hadn't shown up in the office the two days since their return (there was really no need; they were officially on holiday), anxious there would be a confrontation of some sort. Maybe Sheridan had been right: whatever their differences, he should have made an effort to work with him as a team, and he should have tried to console Sheridan on the plane. Yet the accusation that disturbed Danny the most had nothing to do with race or conduct or compassion. It was when Sheridan had asked if he loved his family. He had felt suddenly ashamed, because he had thought of Rachel and Michael, of his father and mother, of his brother and sister, and he had realized that he could not automatically declare, Yes, they're what I live for.

At the benefit dinner, he was seated next to a skeletal old widow named Maggie Hartmann, a major patron to the Huntington. She seemed quite taken by Danny and was chatting jauntily to him. Preoccupied, Danny half listened to her ramble on about the bygone era of Boston theaters, the grand shows they'd had at the Colonial and Wilbur and Majestic; she couldn't understand why no one went to plays anymore; one of the primary reasons she split her time between Boston and New York was her love for the theater, though even the Upper East Side was becoming unlivable. "At least we have those wonderful Korean markets," Mrs. Hartmann said. "Those grocers work so hard, such long hours, and they keep their stores so well stocked and clean. I don't know what I'd do without my Mr. Song. You Koreans are the hardest working people I know."

"Is that so?" Danny said. He was fully attentive to her now.

"Oh, yes. I admire you so much, especially the sacrifices you make for your children. You know that Mr. Song's son is at N.Y.U. and his daughter is at Cornell? Always studying."

"It's astonishing, the opportunities that are there if one is willing to make the effort," Danny told her. He noticed Rachel eavesdropping on the conversation.

"Yes. Absolutely."

"And the corollary to our success is obvious, isn't it?"

"Yes." Mrs. Hartmann smiled. Then she hesitated and said, "Well, I'm not sure I know what you mean."

"Laziness—the real bane of the black and Hispanic underclass. Do you believe that our talent in the sciences and in music is genetic, akin to rhythm or passion? Or maybe we're simply forced to sublimate because our dicks are so small."

"Oh, my."

"Daniel!" Rachel said.

"If you think about it," he told Mrs. Hartmann, "you'll realize that you've just made a colossal idiot of yourself."

Walking out of the Copley Plaza, Rachel was furious. "What's wrong with you? What's happened to you?"

"It's part of growing up—knowing that it no longer matters to be nice. I won't tolerate condescension. You shouldn't, either."

"She was trying to give you a compliment."

"No stereotype is innocent. You can't excuse bigotry because it's well intended."

"God, listen to yourself," Rachel said. "That's all you talk about. This whole thing with Kevin. Everyone's a racist! You've become completely paranoid."

"Are you denying that racism exists?"

Rachel sighed. "Of course I'm not. But the thought of it's taken over your life, it's poisoned you, and that's sadder than anything anyone could ever say or do to you. Don't you see? Racism's not the problem. It's you. You've got no heart, Daniel. You've got no soul."

▪   ▪   ▪

D.R.C.'s Christmas party was held at the Charles Hotel in Harvard Square. All evening, Danny avoided Sheridan, who had come without his wife, Celie. He seemed strangely ebullient, however, greeting people jovially, which sank Danny's hopes: Sheridan must have known something he didn't about the partnership. At the end of the party, Sheridan walked over to him, expansive, friendly. "No hard feelings?" he asked.

"Why would there be?" Danny said hatefully.

"Good." To Danny's amazement, Sheridan hugged him. "Take care of yourself," he said, and left.

Dennis Rhodes signaled to Danny. As he went to the corner to meet him, Danny composed some dignified words with which to tender his resignation. He would have to send out his vita tomorrow so he could arrange interviews immediately after his vacation.

"You know we're not going to announce this until January, but I thought you ought to hear it now." Dennis shook his hand. "You're the new partner. There was never any question about it. Even before the Beal job."

Danny was initially speechless. When he could gather himself, he thanked Dennis for his confidence in him. "When are you going to tell Kevin?" he asked.

"He knows already. Actually, he came to my *house* this morning and demanded an answer."

"I don't understand, then," Danny said. "He looked so . . . happy tonight."

"I thought that was weird, too. Marc Ballinger told me Kevin's behavior was a little erratic. Did he seem erratic to you?"

Danny deliberated his response. "No, nothing out of the ordinary," he finally said.

He told Rachel the news as they pulled out of the hotel's parking garage. She beamed at him. "Does this mean you'll be able to relax in St. John now?"

"I think so," he said.

As they waited to turn left at an intersection, several colleagues and their spouses passed them, honking, wishing them a Merry Christmas. He and Rachel waved, and then Danny swung onto Memorial Drive, alongside the Charles. The river was partially frozen, a foggy film of ice glowing a reflection of the moon. The sky was clear, and there were no other cars on the road, and soon there were glimpses of the downtown Boston skyline. "It's a beautiful night," Rachel said.

"Yeah, it is," Danny said. He was filled with relief and pride and—for the first time in years—genuine affection for Rachel. He moved one hand off the steering wheel to touch her, but then stopped and gripped the wheel again. Ahead of them was a car, going slowly, weaving, no lights. "Drunk driver," he said to Rachel.

They gained on him. "Stay away from the guy," Rachel said.

"I can't help it. He's barely moving."

The driver was bouncing crazily inside the car, lurching for the doors. "What's he doing?" Danny said. It looked like he was rolling down his windows, every single one.

"Isn't that Kevin's car?" Rachel asked.

It was. They got within thirty yards of him, and then, without warning, Sheridan floored it, sped off. Intuitively, Danny knew Sheridan hadn't recognized them. He wasn't running away, he was racing *toward* something.

Danny chased after him.

"Don't," Rachel said. "It's dangerous. Just let him go."

"Put your seat belt on," he told her. He rapidly shifted up to fifth. He thought he might have lost Sheridan—nothing ahead—and then he saw a flash of red brake lights on a curve, a shadowed outline of his car. Sheridan was on a short straightaway now, and he was accelerating, not slowing down for the next bend.

"Jesus," Danny said.

Sheridan's car jumped the curb, flew across the grassy esplanade, and crashed through the railing into the river.

Danny skidded to a halt, jumped out of the car, and ran toward the tangled gap in the railing. He stripped off his overcoat and suit jacket, and dove into the water. For a second there was only blackness, no sensation, no sound, an abyss. Something touched his hands. Mud. It wasn't too deep, twelve feet or so. He surfaced, and the cold seized him, was electric. He dove again, and somehow, though he could see nothing, he found the car almost immediately this time. There was the hood, the windshield, the open driver's window. He reached inside, swept his arm back and forth. Sheridan wasn't there. He was searching from the wrong side—this was the backseat. He lunged into the other window and grabbed Sheridan and struggled to pull him out. He was dead weight, unconscious, unbelievably heavy. Danny used his legs for leverage and pushed upward. They broke the surface. He saw Rachel standing at the railing, screaming at them. He flipped Sheridan over so he was supine and began hauling him to shore. Suddenly Sheridan regained consciousness. He coughed and retched out water. Raspily he hyperventilated for air and clawed at Danny's arm.

"It's okay, I got you, you're safe," Danny said, but Sheridan panicked. He spun around and squeezed Danny in a bear hug, dunking them underwater. Danny kicked his legs, and they bobbed up, but he couldn't break Sheridan's embrace, his arms were pinned. Everything was noisy, the splashing and wrestling—vertiginous, as if he were upside down. It occurred to him that Sheridan might be trying to kill him, take Danny with him. He was so tired, the idea of giving in, sinking into the darkness, was dimly appealing. Sheridan's eyes were wild; he was yelling unintelligibly. Danny swallowed water, strained to keep them afloat. He couldn't last much longer. He tried to recall the Red Cross lifesaving techniques he'd learned as a teenager, the escape from a front head hold. Another memory came to him—a perfect, inviolate rescue. He stretched back, and, as hard as he could, he butted his head into Sheridan's face.

▪   ▪   ▪

YEARS later, he returned to Rosarita Bay with Rachel, Michael, and their daughter, Grace, for his sister's wedding. Lily and the groom, Duncan Roh, were married on the headlands overlooking Rummy Creek, and afterward the reception was held at Duncan's restaurant, Banzai Pipeline, on Main Street.

Danny's parents had flown in from Oahu, where they now lived, and they were becoming fast friends with Mr. and Mrs. Roh, who were Korean and, coincidentally, from Hawaii as well.

Eugene came up to Danny with two mud slides. "I'm in love with this drink," he said, handing one to his brother.

"I think Dad's had a few of these. Look at him." Face flushed red, their father was gesturing animatedly, entertaining their mother and the Rohs with a story. "It's good to see him having a good time," Danny said.

Lily and Duncan were dancing, the kids were running loose, making mischief, and Rachel and Eugene's wife, Janet, were chatting quietly at a table together.

"I've been thinking about taking the family on a trip to Korea," Danny told Eugene. "What do you think? Want to come along?"

"I don't know how Janet would feel about that. She's never had any interest in going, you know. Too bitter about her mom's relatives."

"What about just you, then?"

"I'll talk to her," Eugene said. "Who knows. Maybe she'll come."

Rachel ambled up to Danny. "Dance?" she said. She took his hand and led him to the dance floor. It was a slow song, and they shuffled and swayed tiredly to the music. They were both exhausted. "How's it feel to be back?" she asked.

"Strange," he said. "It's been a while." He couldn't believe that Eugene had moved back to Rosarita Bay, and that Lily had never left.

"It's a nice little town," Rachel said, "but I think I'd go crazy here. It's not Boston."

Danny was still at D.R.C. He had seen Sheridan only once more, a few days after their struggle in the river. He had visited him at McLean's, the psychiatric hospital, where

Sheridan had asked to be taken. They had nothing really to say to each other, but Sheridan appreciated that he came. He actually didn't mind being there, he told Danny. For once, he could rest. Sheridan had not been trying to drown him, Danny knew then, and he decided that maybe Sheridan wasn't that much of a bigot; he had been, then and all along, just terrified.

As he and Rachel danced, Danny watched his son approach the floor, escorting a girl on his arm. She was about the same age as Michael—sixteen—and she was a little heartbreaker, blond, in a tight burgundy dress. Michael raised his left arm, lightly pressed his right hand into the small of the girl's back, and launched her into a waltz. He danced well, though he was a bit stiff. Michael caught Danny looking at him. He grinned and gave his father a wink, and Danny marveled at the simple, pure joy of seeing his son's face, which was, he had to admit, becoming remarkably like his own.